# Winters'
# Resonance

Jenifer Lynn

ISBN-13: 978-0-578-40485-1

# DEDICATION

For Rinzen and Xander.

# ACKNOWLEDGMENTS

Without Erin, I would never have taken the time to write
this. The constant encouragement didn't hurt either.
Also, my husband Jess, who created an amazing world with
amazing characters, and then allowed me to take the reins.

# PROLOGUE - 1985

The crunching sound of struts past their prime joined the cacophony of wind and engine as the wood-paneled 1976 Dodge Aspen sped along the floor of the canyon. The sun, lazy at this late hour, couldn't be bothered to do more than skim the tops of the mountains, leaving the station wagon in a premature twilight.

"Do you guys feel a wobble?"

Julia Winters looked at her big brother and rolled her eyes dramatically. She saw a hint of a smile before he sighed and said, "No, Dad."

"Dad, if you're worried about another flat tire, why don't we get a hotel room and look at it in the morning?" Julia suggested, her voice a little too bright. The landscape had been eerie and flat for what felt like forever, but now the mountains surged up around them bringing to mind giants that were just waiting for the right moment to pounce. The girl shivered and brushed away her overactive imagination, "Please?"

"Sweetie, we just don't have the money for another hotel," Mr. Winters said. "Plus, do you really want to wait another whole day to get to," he paused, cleared his throat and affected his best announcer voice. "The Happiest Place on Earth?" He coughed, voice falling back to a more natural cadence, "If you kids catch some Z's we'll be there before you know it."

Julia smiled and elbowed her brother. "Gene, did you hear that?" she asked, eight-year-old enthusiasm breaking through the darkness surrounding the car. "Disneyland tomorrow!"

Gene didn't look up from his magazine and shrugged. "Yay," he said.

Julia saw her dad's face in the rearview mirror. He was watching Gene, expression pensive. She turned back to her brother. "I hear they have a haunted house with real ghosts, Gene. Doesn't that sound fun?"

"Sure," said Gene, turning the page on his magazine.

"I bet there's an arcade!" She elbowed him again, grinning. "Maybe they'll have that Last Starfighter game!"

Gene brightened, "That would be awesome."

Mr. Winters caught her eye in the rearview and winked at her, smiling. Then the wheel jerked under his hands and his smile faded. "You sure you don't feel that? I swear there's a wobble."

"No, Dad," Julia told him. "We didn't feel anything."

Gene put his magazine in the pocket on the back of the empty passenger seat next to a recently used tire iron, giving up on the remaining light, and looked around at their surroundings for the first time since they'd crossed into the foothills. "Wow," he breathed, craning his head to see the tops of the canyon and what was left of the sunset light. Julia saw him shudder, and he reached for her hand. "Dad, let's find a place to stop, somewhere with lights."

Julia nodded emphatically. "And food!"

"But especially lights," Gene said.

"And pie!" she added.

Gene smiled at her, squeezing her hand before turning his eyes back to the shadows that moved around the car, getting darker by the minute.

They came out of the canyon just as the sun was setting. Julia sat with her legs to her chest, fussing with a loose string on her wool leg warmers. Gene was fidgeting as well, scanning all directions, looking for signs of civilization.

"Look!" Mr. Winters said, pointing to an ancient looking billboard. "Truck stop, this exit!"

Julia's stomach growled in response, she could already taste the French fries.

They crested the top of a tall foothill and saw the dim lights of the truck stop at the peak of the next hill. It looked nearly deserted, only one semi in the lot, but the lights were on, and as they got closer, a red neon "Open" sign shown in the window.

The station wagon's engine protested being cut off, rumbling grumpily before it quieted. Mr. Winters got out and stretched, back cracking. Gene had tossed on his Converse high tops, not bothering to lace them, and he grabbed Julia's hand, pulling her out his side and hustling them to the door of the restaurant. "C'mon, Dad," Gene called, yanking open the door and pushing Julia inside.

Julia turned back, laughing at her brother's antics until she noticed his expression as he stared out into the falling darkness. "Gene?" she asked, tentative. She reached out for his arm, feeling his tenseness flow into her as shadows encroached on their father's form. "Gene, what's wrong?" The shadows were darker than they should be, she thought. Moving unnaturally in the waning light. Swarming and circling her dad as he made his way all too slowly to the door. "What is it?" she whispered.

"Hey!" a shrill voice made both of them jump and turn to face the waitress that had appeared behind them. Dyed orange wisps of hair clashed soundly with her bright pink dress, buttons stretched to the point of no return across her plentiful torso. "Wanna booth or are ya gonna sit at the counter?" Garishly painted lips parted in a smile that told them clearly that they had arrived far too close to closing time for her liking.

Julia choked back a yelp as hands fell on her shoulders. "A booth will be fine, thanks," Mr. Winters said.

She relaxed, leaning back and looking at him with relief before turning back to the waitress. "Do you have pie?"

"It's been in the case all day," the waitress grumbled. "But you can have it if you want it."

"Appetizing," Gene said absently. His eyes were back on the play of light and shadow in the parking lot. It looked somewhat less ominous now, simply small swarms of insects invading the light of the single yellow halogen lamp. Julia threaded her fingers through his, pulling him to follow the woman in the unfortunate pink dress.

"We close in fifteen minutes," the waitress said as the family seated themselves. "Fryers aren't up anymore, so your choices are limited." She tossed menus down in front of them and pulled out a notepad. "What'd'ya want?"

"Um," Mr. Winters scanned the menu quickly, sharing a look with his children before ordering, "Three burgers, three cokes, and two slices of pie, please?"

The waitress scratched their hasty order onto her notepad and disappeared in a flurry of starch and stale cigarette smoke without another word.

"Charming place," Gene said, reaching out to fiddle with the disposable tin ashtray that looked like it probably should have been disposed of many months ago.

"This is awesome!" Julia said, staring at the tiny tabletop jukebox next to the wall. "Dad, can I have a quarter?" She held out her hand and gave him her best Daddy's Girl smile.

He obliged, "I haven't seen one of these since your mom and I were dating." He smiled eyes lighting up with a fond, bittersweet nostalgia. "She loved Patsy Cline," he said.

Julia typed in a number and Cline's voice reached out through the ancient speakers. "Did she like this one?"

Her dad smiled, "She loved it, kiddo."

It had been over a year since their mother had died. Every time Julia thought about it, really thought about it, she felt a churning lake of black water open under her feet and threaten to pull her down and drown her. So she didn't think about it, choosing to focus instead on trying to keep her brother from falling into his own pool of sadness. He was having a much harder time pretending like everything was still okay, and there were days she thought she may not be strong enough to pull him free. Right now seemed like one of those times, he had stiffened at the first mention of their mom, a dark and angry look in his eye as he flipped the dirty ashtray over and over with building violence.

Plates and glasses were unceremoniously dropped in front of them, burgers that looked like they'd been thrown together as a part of some kind of ring toss game, melting pie, and cokes with no ice and no straw. "That'll be thirteen dollars, sixty-eight cents," the waitress said and held out her meaty hand.

Their dad shared another look with them, and pulled

out his wallet, giving her a ten and a five. "Keep the change," he said.

She rolled her eyes at him and walked away.

"We should probably eat fast," Mr. Winters said, smirking.

The burgers were about as good as they looked, but Julia ate hers without complaint. Gene picked at his food, casting nervous glances at the big picture window that faced the parking lot. It was full dark now, thick solid blackness had replaced the separated moving shadows of earlier. The effect wasn't any less ominous, and Julia was in no hurry to leave the bright fluorescent lights of the restaurant despite how unwelcome they felt.

"Well," Mr. Winters said, getting up and slipping a couple more dollars under his half-full glass of coke. "Ready?"

Gene slid out of his seat, setting his narrow shoulders. "Bet Jules and I can beat you to the car," he challenged their father, flashing a smile that Julia could see was forced.

Mr. Winters seemed a little confused as well, leading the kids to the front door. The lights in the front of the building were off. "Race?"

"Yeah!" Gene said, stopping them at the door and taking a starting line stance. "Ready? Set? Go!"

Gene grabbed Julia's hand, pulling her behind him. Their dad was on their heels, panting and laughing as they crossed the lot to their car. The three of them reached the doors at the same time, Gene throwing her in the back seat, diving in after and reaching to push down the each of the locks. Julia saw his hands were shaking as he locked the driver's side door after their dad got settled. His smile from earlier had been replaced by a pale determination.

"Let's go, Dad," Gene said.

"Yep, just gotta get my keys here-"

There was a knock on the driver's side window. Gene jumped, throwing an arm around Julia and squeezing them both into the centermost part of the back seat.

"Let's go, Dad," Gene said again. "Seriously."

"Can you help us?" came a muffled monotone through the closed window, and then another knock.

Their dad had finally found his keys, slipping them into the ignition before he acknowledged the figures outside the car. "They're kids," he said with a slight surprise in his tone.

"Dad, we have to go," Gene said.

Julia tried to get a look at who was at the door, despite Gene's tight grip and her overwhelming urge to close her eyes until they were back on the road. Two figures, one just a little too tall to see his face, the other short enough to peer into the car at her father. Dark sweatshirts with the hoods up mostly obscured their faces, but Julia could assume from the straw-colored braids that the shorter one was a girl. They couldn't be much older than she and Gene.

"Come on," the other child said, the girl this time, in the same dead monotone. "People are supposed to help other people, mister."

"Help us," said the other. "We need a ride."

"Dad!" Gene shouted as their dad reached for the lock on his door. "Let's just go. Please." The strength in Gene's voice was faltering, and Julia could feel him trembling next to her.

"I don't like this, Daddy," Julia said, her own voice small and scared. "Gene's right, we should-"

"Please, mister," the hooded girl cut her off. "It's scary out here."

Julia watched as her dad reached for the lock again, her eyes trailing from his hand to the face outside the window. The hood was turned to her now and she could clearly see the girl's face shadowed within. Pale and drawn, smudged with dirt, her lips were dry and chapped and they turned up in a slight mechanical smile when Julia's gaze finally reached her eyes. Ink black eyes with no pupil, no color, no life, stared back at her with a kind of triumph as her father pulled up the lock.

"Guys, it's fine," their dad said, pulling the handle on his door. His own voice was faded, dazed. "What kind of person would I be if I left two kids stranded in a-"

Julia screamed and Gene shouted, "Dad! No!" as the two figures pulled him from the car almost faster than their eyes could process. There was a shout, then a sickening wet thud and the hooded faces appeared at the back window. A pale hand snaked through the open front door and reached for the lock on Gene's side.

Gene pushed Julia back against her door, lifting his sneakered feet to kick at the hand. Julia heard a crunch, but the kid didn't flinch as he reached the lock and pulled up. Gene did the same on Julia's side, opening the door and pushing her out onto the cement. She barely caught herself before falling face-first into the asphalt, rolling out of the way so Gene could follow her. She heard the tire iron clatter to the ground with him, then looked past him under the car. Julia only had time to take in her father's legs and feet laying on the ground, and how the cement seemed more red than black, shining in the halogen light before Gene hauled her to her feet.

"Julia!" Gene shouted at her, pulling her away from the car. "We've got to run!"

The taller figure, pale face and those same ink-black eyes now visible, was crawling through the back seat, attention locked on Julia. The shorter one was making her way around the back of the car with something wet and dripping in her hand.

Julia was frozen in place, "What about Dad?"

Gene pulled harder, bruising her arm. "We've got to go, Jules!" But the taller figure was spilling out of the back seat, closing in on them. Gene stepped in front of Julia, raising the tire iron and hitting him across the side of his head. A sickening crunch and he fell out of the car to the cement, but he was back on his feet a moment later to continue his blank-faced pursuit. Her brother swung again, this time catching the kid in the cheek, bones caving in. The boy didn't stumble, he just kept coming as black blood ran down the side of his face.

Gene cursed, grabbing better hold of Julia and ran.

Julia was fighting shock, clinging to the ordinary feeling of her feet hitting the ground and her burning lungs to keep her from crumbling into a pile of sobbing screams. Gene was yelling at her to go faster, and she really tried, but she was smaller than he was. Her legs were shorter and she just couldn't keep up.

"Jules!" They were across the parking lot now, standing on the old highway. Gene kept dragging her along, she could hear the relentless footfalls of the hooded kids behind them. "There's a truck!" He pointed at lights that were probably a half mile off at the crest of the next hill, a semi-truck heading east. "Get to that truck, Jules." Gene pulled her around, leaning down to her, his voice low and urgent. "You have to run. You have to get safe. Now go."

He let go of her, shoving her in the direction of the truck before he turned to face the black-eyed figures coming toward them.

"Don't look back, Jules," Gene shouted back at her. "Just run."

A last look at her big brother's silhouette as he raised the tire iron, then Julia turned and ran. Tears blurred her vision, turning the oncoming headlights into bright halos.

At the bottom of the hill, she began waving her arms and letting the screams that had been held in rip from her throat. The truck's brakes drowned out her voice as the monstrous wheels came to a stop beside her on the road.

"-an ankle biter wandering around out here, gonna check it out," a woman's voice floated down to her through the opening passenger side door. A sharp click and jumbled reply from the CB radio, then, "What the hell are you doin' kid?"

Julia pulled herself up into the cab with shaking hands and leg muscles that were close to giving out. "My brother! My dad! Please, you have to help them!" Julia pointed to the top of the hill where the faint glow of the single halogen identified the truck stop.

The woman in the driver's seat took in Julia's appearance and hit the gas, urging the truck to climb the hill as best as she could. "What happened, sweetie?" she asked Julia.

"These kids," she said. "They just-" she broke off as the parking lot came into view. Their car was still there, passenger side facing them with the back door wide open, parking lot deserted. "Where's my brother?" she whispered.

"Stay here," said the driver as she parked diagonally across two aisles of parking spaces. "I'm going to go check the car."

Julia protested, but the woman got out and walked around to the driver's side of their family station wagon. She saw the color drain from the woman's face as her gaze landed on the ground. She looked up sharply, scanning the lot, but apparently seeing nothing. Julia opened the door and climbed down, but the driver was there to stop her from going any further.

"No, honey, you don't wanna go over there." The woman wrapped an arm around her gently, leading her back to the door.

"But my brother," she said, her voice climbing in volume. "Gene. Gene!" She grabbed the woman's shirt, "I need to find my brother!"

"How old is your brother, honey?" the trucker asked.

"He's fourteen."

"Ok, well he's not here now. Let's get you back into the truck and I'll take you someplace safe, okay?"

Julia struggled against the woman's hold, yelling her brother's name into the silence, hearing nothing but her own voice echo back. After a moment, she let the driver buckle her into the passenger seat. Dimly she heard the CB radio click and the woman ask if there were any "smokies" on the line. She watched with drying tears as the parking lot disappeared in the side mirror. They were headed east, back the way they had come, leaving the "Happiest Place on Earth" far behind them.

# PART ONE
## CHAPTER ONE - 2000

"Julia!"

Tabitha's shriek reached through the fog of sleep into Julia's brain, found the box holding her hangover, and tipped it over. Dehydration and regret oozed out, running in rivulets through her system introducing cottonmouth, a headache, and something dire in her stomach, that may or may not last the whole day.

"Julia, damnit, your cat is in my room again!"

Julia cracked an eye open, testing the waters before allowing the other eye to follow suit. A beam of dust-filled sunlight spilled through a broken blind, landing on a stuffed donkey near her head. "Is the cat rearranging the furniture, Arthur?" she asked the donkey. "Running an illegal gambling operation?"

"Julia!" came the shriek again. She rolled her eyes at the donkey, before pulling herself from under the covers. The wood floor was cool under her bare feet, and it perked her senses just enough to stave off the spinning sensation that threatened her equilibrium.

Her roommate was standing down the hall, facing through the open doorway into her bedroom. "He's a cat, not a mountain lion, Tab," Julia whispered, brushing past Tabitha in her business suit and into the immaculately clean bedroom. Julia took a blissful moment to ponder how hard it would be to find a new roommate. A digital clock on the nightstand read 7:30 am.

"Don't call me that," Tabitha snapped. "And he's not just a cat, he's a demon cat."

Julia's eyes crawled up to the stucco ceiling. "Just because he doesn't like you..." she trailed off, catching sight of a long striped grey tail under the bed. "Come here, Rufus." The tail disappeared and a second later a white and grey nose poked out from under the perfectly made duvet. "Come on, kitty." The cat leisurely stretched then padded over to Julia. She bent down and was met with a loud purr as Rufus curled up in her arms, closing his eyes when she stroked the soft fur between his ears. "So vicious."

"He's a demon," Tabitha repeated, giving Julia a wide berth as she passed by. As soon as it was clear, her roommate stepped into her room and slammed the door.

Julia looked down at the cat, sleepily purring in her arms. "You just have discerning taste, don't you?" Rufus opened one green eye, then yawned before squirming to get down. He meowed up at her and led her into the kitchen, circling his food bowl. Julia smirked, "Or maybe you only tolerate the humans that feed you."

Fifteen minutes later Tabitha breezed out the door without a goodbye, and Julia was sitting down at her computer with two slices of dry toast and a cup of ginger ale. As the screech of the modem came to a conclusion, she reached over to flip on the police scanner. Typical morning chatter filled the room, and she knocked the volume down slightly to appease her throbbing head. There were a dozen new emails, mostly from the paranormal newsgroups she belonged to. Two emails from her aunt that she promptly marked as read, a couple submissions to her website, and one email from the Grand River Tribune about making the switch to digital photography. She glared at the overpriced Canon Powershot that sat on the end of her desk next to her beloved Pentax. There was no accounting for taste when it came to newspaper editors.

She was just about to open one the first of the website submissions, titled "Spooky Cemetery Encounter" when the tone of the police scanner chatter shifted. No one ever sounded panicked on the police scanner, but after years of listening, Julia had learned to pick up on those subtle shifts that meant they weren't just talking about a petty theft or a bathroom break. She turned up the volume, listened for a moment, and abandoned the remaining toast to rush to her room. Moments later she was wearing jeans and a button up shirt as she sped through the house, finding shoes, keys, and finally her cameras. She picked up the digital, giving herself a moment to scowl, then picked up the Pentax, throwing both into her camera bag. Waving absently to Rufus, who watched her with abject disinterest as she disappeared out the door.

Detective Jonathan Cole tilted his head to the side, a futile attempt to loosen a knot behind his shoulder blade. Sleep had eluded him until fifteen minutes before the call had come in, and his body was making its displeasure evident. He ran a hand back through hair he'd forgotten to comb and pulled a notebook from his worn jacket.

"Okay Mrs. Hammond," He said, turning his attention back to the elderly neighbor who had made the 9-1-1 call. "You said you heard shouting this morning at what time?"

"7:30, it know was 7:30 because they had just done the weather on the morning news with that nice young man, Jesse. He said the weather was supposed to be a little cold, and he was right."

Cole took his jacket off, offering it to the woman. She smiled and began the laborious task of finding where her arms fit into the oversized coat. He held it for her patiently, scanning the scene. To his right, Sergeant Biggs, a woman that generally wore a wicked smile to go with her dark sense of humor, was uncharacteristically serious as she helped another officer string up the yellow tape. A green Ford hatchback caught his attention as it pulled up to his left, parking across the street from the crime scene. A slender young woman slid out of the driver's seat, silvery blonde hair obscuring her face as she leaned back into the car to grab a large camera bag. As an afterthought, she reached in and pulled a lanyard from the rearview mirror, tossing it around her neck. He turned back to his witness, hearing the shutter of the girl's camera begin to snap.

"And then what, Mrs. Hammond?"

"Well I looked out the window," she continued, "And I saw three young people wearing hooded sweatshirts, and they were taking little Timothy out of the house."

"Was he struggling?" Cole asked. Out of the corner of his eye, he saw a camera flash, then heard the girl curse under her breath.

"No, he was just kind of limp, and that didn't seem right." The elderly woman shook her head, hands knotted into the front of her shirt. "And then I called the 9-1-1, but my phone is on the wall in the kitchen, and I

15

can't see the road from the kitchen, so after the 9-1-1 girl told me that you people were on your way, I went back into the living room, but I didn't see those kids or little Timothy anywhere."

"Do you know how old Timothy is, Ms. Hammond?" Cole asked, noticing that the intermittent shutter clicks of the blonde girl's camera were getting closer.

"He's in college, I think. Community college."

Cole nodded, making note that they weren't looking for a child as previously assumed. "Okay, what happened next?"

"Well, then I went over to make sure that Mr. Knox was okay." She went pale. "And he wasn't. He was on the floor, and - and there was so much blood…" She looked up at him, eyes wide. "He said they had black eyes. That the kids that took Tim had black eyes."

"He was conscious when you found him, ma'am?"

She nodded, her attention falling down the road where the ambulance had been moments before. "Is Mr. Knox going to be okay?"

His gaze followed hers. The victim had been slashed repeatedly across the chest and belly. If Mr. Knox had been conscious, then some of the wounds must have been superficial, but the amount of blood at the scene told him that many were deep and dangerous. "I will make sure someone keeps you updated, Ms. Hammond." He squeezed her shoulder. "Thank you for your time. Why don't you get back in the house where it's warm?"

The woman nodded and slid out of his jacket, handing it to him with a, "Thank you, young man." He turned back to the house and noticed that the clicking shutter had fallen silent. A quick scan of the scene revealed that the girl had disappeared.

Julia's stomach turned when she reached the victim's

living room. The rich iron smell of fresh blood was degrading into the sticky slowing smell of death. She put the digital camera in her bag, and pulled the film camera out, adjusting the settings for the low lighting. The comfortable trigger leading into the automatic movement of her thumb to advance the film helped to detach her from the scene in front of her - and from what she had just overheard during the neighbor's interview. She took a few more pictures, not sure what she would get, but prompted by her obsession to keep shooting. She was near the end of her roll when she heard the voice behind her.

"I'm not sure what kind of credentials you have, but I'm fairly certain they don't allow this much access."

She stood straight and tempered her face to be friendly, but solemn in light of the setting, and turned to face the owner of the voice. He was leaning casually against the doorframe, and she wondered how long he had been watching her. He was attractive, if somewhat unkempt which was to be expected this early in the morning. No uniform, but she could see the flash of a badge on his belt and the butt of a handgun under his jacket. She slipped her lanyard over her head and handed it to him.

"Julia Winters with The Grand River Tribune?" he said, looking at the front and back of her press card.

"Freelance, actually," she said.

He cocked his head, studying her with slight amusement in his pale green eyes. "Do freelancers always sneak past the police line, or is that just a Julia Winters thing?"

She put her Pentax in her bag, snapping a picture of him in the process to finish up the roll, then smiled at him. "It's a good journalist thing." He handed her ID back to her, and she slipped the lanyard back over her head.

"Well, Miss Winters," he said stepping out of the doorway. "You had probably better vanish before the uniforms find you in here." He lifted his hands. "Your creds aren't much good here and I cannot protect you."

She nodded a thank you and slipped past him out the door. Two uniformed officers were hovering by their car, waiting for forensics, and she was able to get back to safety without issue. Once she was in her car, she took a moment to put her aching head against the steering wheel. She allowed her brain to process what she had heard, and her heart rate sped up, thumping pain in her chest. The old woman's voice echoed in her mind.

"He said they had black eyes."

\*\*\*

# From the Message Boards

## Topic: Tallahassee BEK Story

**Forgotten1968**  *5-25-1999, 1:22pm*
They've taken him to a better place.

**Raccoon**  *5-25-1999, 1:24pm*
....what?

**Forgotten1968**  *5-25-1999, 1:30pm*
The young man who was chosen by the Children. They have taken him to a better world.

**Raccoon**  *5-26-1999, 3:00pm*
You've gotta be fucking kidding me...
\*\*\*

# CHAPTER TWO

*The train didn't understand the concept of time. It sped along on rails that weren't constrained by the concepts of matter and motion. Through nonexistent forests, under invisible mountains, and over lakes made of thought and willpower.*

*The man that sat on the dusty floor of the empty railcar playing solitaire with a cigarette clamped between his teeth did, however, understand these concepts, and he was beginning to wonder if he would make it to his destination before he ran out of smokes.*

By noon Julia had dropped her film canister off for development and transferred the photos from the Canon to her computer. She chose two pictures of the outside of the house, attaching them to an email and adding the tagline "Man in critical care after brutal attack. Witness says victim's adult son was taken from house by kids with black eyes." She added a note to her editor in the email, saying that she had been ousted from the property before she was able to get any worthwhile interviews, but that she would try to follow up with the victim if he regained consciousness. She hit send and watched in a daze as the upload bar began crawling across the screen. The police chatter had been mundane white noise since she got back from the crime scene. No sign of the missing man according to the authorities.

With a sigh, she minimized the upload window and took stock of her unread emails. New messages in the newsgroups for "Dimensional Portals" and "Paranormal Disappearances," and an apparent sighting of a sasquatch in a Wal-Mart in the "Cryptozoology" thread. She skipped past those, landing on the two website submission emails she had received during the night. Scanning through, she saw the usual preamble of introduction and "This actually happened" followed by a clumsily written account of something ghostly happening to a couple of teens in a cemetery. She read through it a couple times, debating the veracity, before highlighting and copying it into a new window. The second email, coming from a yourmom1999@netscape.com, a crudely written encounter with a "suckubus". She deleted it without bothering to finish it.

The website she ran was not much more than an accumulation of paranormal stories, but it got a lot of traffic, and the submissions were upwards of 300 after only two years running it. It was nothing fancy, a black background with a few terrible looking ghost animations, and over a dozen different categories ranging from Cryptozoology to Hauntings, and a message board. She copied the new submission into the "Cemetery" category, crediting the author as requested.

Black-Eyed Kids had their own category. Stories from as early as the 1930s, but almost always the same. Two or three kids in what appeared to be dark hooded clothing asking to be invited into a home, or asking for a ride somewhere. The feeling of being compelled to help them, until the potential victim realized that the kids had blackened, burnt-out eyes and was able to break free of whatever thrall they'd seemingly cast. Julia chewed on her lip indecisively for a full five minutes before typing up a quick account of the detective's interview she had heard that morning. She added "**Not Yet Verified**" to the top of the story before submitting it to the site. Julia glared at that statement for a few moments, then after checking her upload to the paper, only 25% complete, she resigned herself to slightly more extreme measures of gathering information.

Winter in the town of Grand River had given up the ghost about two weeks before, allowing for spring to take hold. The thawing ground broke open to greens, the smell of decaying leaves mingled with the distinct scents of river and lake battling the surface ice for the first time in months. It was refreshing but brisk as Julia walked from her car across the parking lot to the three-story building that had served the small town as the hospital for nearly 80 years.

She knew the building all too well from her childhood, and not much had changed. The Intensive Care Unit was on the second floor of the east wing. Getting there wasn't difficult, but she wasn't sure exactly what the plan was after that. Three nurses were standing at their station, not quite engrossed enough in conversation and paperwork to let her pass by without interference. She hovered near the waiting room, pondering her next step. The old, steal a lab coat and pretend to be official only worked in the movies, and these nurses didn't look like they would be easily conned into believing she was family. She was preparing to channel her inner ninja and just go for it when the strong smell of vending machine coffee assaulted her senses.

"You were far stealthier this morning," said a voice

from the direction of the burnt coffee. She recognized it and closed her eyes taking a deep breath before turning to face the detective.

"Nurses are scarier than cops," she said and offered a smile.

He laughed loudly, surprising her and earning a glare from the nurses. He schooled his features, nodded to the stern women, and gestured for Julia to follow him into the empty family waiting room. She sat down at a table meant for board games and coloring books and the detective sat across from her, setting his foul smelling brew between them.

"Would you like some coffee?" he asked.

She shook her head, "No thank you, Detective..." She left the missing name hanging.

"Cole," he said, offering his hand. "Jonathan Cole."

She took his hand. "I'm not being interrogated, am I?"

He smiled, showing laugh lines around his eyes. She guessed him to be in his thirties. "No. But despite my admiration of your tenacity Miss Winters, I have to warn you that it's not legal for the press to be harassing the victim."

She nodded, "I understand." She paused, raising her eyebrows slightly. "So... he's still alive then? Will he pull through?"

Cole scowled at her, but there was amusement in his eyes. "Miss Winters..."

"It's not for the paper," she said quickly. "Honestly. I just want to see if he's going to be okay."

Cole sighed. "He's in and out of consciousness," he admitted. "The doctor seems tentatively hopeful."

"That's good," Julia said, feeling a rush of relief for the stranger. "Has he said anything?"

Cole's brows drew together. "Why, if not for the

paper?"

"I just-" she broke off, chewing on her lip before throwing caution to the wind. "It's just that I heard the neighbor mention kids with black eyes…"

He blinked. "Yeah, she did."

"Has the victim said anything more?"

He was watching her intently now, pale green eyes narrowed. "What do you know about the attackers, Miss Winters?"

"Nothing," Julia paused, feeling a buzz at her side as her pager went off. "Nothing really." She took her pager from her pocket and looked at the number. "I'm sorry - I should go."

The detective stood with her, putting his hand out to stop her. "He has mentioned them again," he said. "He's not overly coherent, but he's been mumbling something about black eyes." He handed her a card, "If there is anything you can tell me, Miss Winters, please call." He caught her gaze with an earnestness that nearly made her second guess her decision to bail.

"I will," She nodded, taking the card and slipping it into the front pocket of her camera bag. "Thank you."


There was a payphone on the sidewalk near where she had parked. The brisk air helped to wash away the stifled feeling of the hospital. The phone rang four times before it picked up.

"Jules," the voice intoned on the other end of the line with a slow mock disinterest. "Your horribly grotesque photographs are ready for you."

She smiled. "Hi, Devin. How are you?"

"Utterly disgusted," he said. "What the ever-loving hell were you shooting this morning?"

"You don't want to know," she said. "Be there in ten."

"I will be waiting for you with the most baited of breath," Devin drawled before the disconnecting click.

The shop was empty but for Devin who was slumped over the counter, chin resting heavily in his long-fingered, perfectly manicured hand. He looked up when she walked in, giving her a lazy smile. "Exciting morning, Jules?"

"That's one word for it," Julia said. She set her camera bag on the counter, then hopped up to sit next to it. "Was there anything interesting in the photos?"

He cocked a dark brow at her, "Interesting? Do you mean the ones with copious amounts of blood splatter or the one with the attractive older gentleman with the gun in his pants?"

She nudged him, "Either. And you know what I mean."

He sighed, pushing himself up from the counter to his full height. "I didn't see anything spooky, Spooky." He pulled an envelope from a drawer, "But have a gander yourself."

She flipped open the envelope, rapidly scanning each gruesome photo.

"What's wrong?" Devin draped an arm around her, leaning in to look over her shoulder. "You're on edge."

Julia got to the end of the photos, the hastily taken image of the detective, and finding nothing out of the ordinary she sighed heavily and put them back in the envelope. "The victim, he's not completely awake yet - but he keeps talking about kids with black eyes."

"Oh." Devin took his arm off her shoulders. "Shit."

"I mean, nothing really tangible or anything," she said.

"Yeah, Jules, but you've got a closet full of baggage on your shoulders," he peered closely at her face, dismayed, "oh, and under your eyes." He clapped his hands together and reached under the counter, pulling out a well-used 'Be Back Soon' sign and slapping it on the door. "We need to have day drinks. This is stressful." He offered his hand to Julia, helping her off the counter before leading her back out to the sidewalk and locking up behind them. "Watch the store, would you, Jerry?"

A pile of rags sitting next to the mouth of the alley near the Photo Shack shifted, rolling forward and a wrinkled, weathered, but friendly face peeked out. "You got it, boss," the man said and gave them a toothsome grin. Devin gave the man a thumbs up before linking arms with Julia and walking them down the street toward his apartment.

*The man on the train had run out of cigarettes. His muscles were taught - on edge - and a dull pain had begun to throb in his left foot. He alternated between sitting and standing, restlessly fiddling with his zippo - lighting it to see in the dark but there was nothing in the train car but sand and straw. However, the flashing lights as they passed … whatever it was they were traveling past … were beginning to slow down. He reached out, putting his hand on the heavy sliding door. It was ice cold. He hesitated a moment before stretching and plopping back down in the corner. It obviously wasn't quite time for him to get off yet.*

By the second drink, the conversation had lightened, and Devin had Julia smiling and laughing. By the third drink, Devin dramatically flopped backward on his couch and announced that the Photo Shack was officially closed for the day. By the fourth drink, the light outside the windows had dimmed past sunset levels, and Julia stood up to go home.

"Are you sure you don't want to stay, Jules?" Devin asked, pouring himself another drink. "We could play dirty Pictionary and make out platonically."

Julia laughed. "Tempting, but some other time, I've got work to do at home."

He looked up, brows furrowed. "Do you need a ride?"

She ruffled his hair and threw her camera bag over her shoulder. "Not from you, Lushy McDrunkenpants."

He snickered and waved as she went out the door.

Her car was parked in front of The Photo Shack which was, like most things in the small town of Grand River, within walking distance from Julia's apartment. She briefly entertained the thought of driving the quick five blocks, but guilt and better judgment won out and she found herself pulling her thin cardigan around her to fight off the deepening cold of the early spring night.

The certainty that she was being followed sank in just past the halfway point between her home and Devin's. Tendrils of fear licked up her spine, urging her forward. She sped up, hearing the echoing footsteps behind her pick up the pace. She turned a corner and chanced a glance back toward the Photo Shack. Two shadows, medium height, wearing hooded sweatshirts with the hoods up. She couldn't see their faces, but she had the distinct feeling that their gazes were zeroed in on her. She was three blocks from home, but when she heard them take the turn and continue to follow her, she broke into a run, slip on shoes slapping against the broken sidewalk. She stumbled twice before the light of her apartment complex chased away a little of the terror. She ran past the haphazardly manicured bushes in front of her building, down the open-air hallway to her apartment door. She threw it open, feeling the flaming fire of demons on her heels, and flung herself into the kitchen. Tabitha was there, warpath written all over her face.

"You left the computer online, Julia," she said. "What if someone important was trying to call?"

"I'm sorry," Julia breathed, locking the deadbolt behind her. The fear wasn't leaving as fast as it should. The warm lights of home were chilled by Tabitha's dark glare. "I had to upload to the paper, and I had to pick up some photos."

"By 'photos' do you mean 'gin' because that's what you smell like," Tabitha said.

Anger flared, replacing the fear. "It's been a long damned day, Tab," Julia snapped. "What I do with my downtime is none of your business."

"It is if you forget your responsibilities here!" Tabitha shouted.

"If by responsibilities, you mean, 'turning off the computer so your dipshit boyfriend can call' then I'm just really not making that a prio-"

A soft knock at the door cut through her words and sent a shock of ice through her heart.

"See what you did?" Tabitha hissed as she headed toward the door. Another knock sounded. "Neighbors are pissed now thanks to all your drunken shouting."

"Tabitha, don't-"

But it was too late. Her roommate swung the door open, a wide, fake smile on her face and an apology on her lips. The hooded teenagers with the fully black eyes and blank faces on the other side of the threshold didn't give her a chance to say anything. One knife dug deep into her stomach, another slashed across her throat. Her fake smile morphed into a genuine grimace of pain and fear as she fell to the ground, hands trying instinctively and futilely to stop the flow of blood pooling in the entryway.

# CHAPTER THREE

Julia's head ached and her mouth was dry. Devin and his cursed strong drinks, she thought, dimly. Her body was stiff, and when she tried to stretch to work out the kinks, she found herself unable to move. Her waking mind, having hidden in the background trying to get more rest, took notice and came rushing toward the front of her consciousness. A pinprick of awareness widening in aperture until the world was loud and painful and bright around her.

She was standing on a wooden platform, bound at the ankles, waist, and chest to what looked like a support beam. Cool metal against her cheek. Her hands were tied to something warm, and with a jolt, she realized she wasn't alone. She looked up and saw the battered face of a young man looking down at her through half-closed eyes. Revelations collided with realizations in unpleasant waves as she took in the rest of the scene.

She was six feet above the ground, tied in part to a metal pole, and in part to a young man who appeared to be only half-conscious. Her hands were roped to his, and when she tried pulling against him, he didn't respond. The platform at their feet was wide, and she imagined scaffolding underneath it to keep them steady as she began to struggle. Her movements jostled the man and he groaned, blood dripping from his mouth and onto the top of her head. She craned her neck as much as she could to see past the platform, and that's when the mind-numbing terror threatened to send her consciousness back to the back of her brain where it was safe.

Eight teens, wearing dark hooded sweatshirts surrounded them, staring silently up at them. They each held torches, the orange lights flickering in their black shark-like eyes. The memory of what happened after she left Devin's house came flooding back in all too vivid glory. Tabitha was dead, she was certain, and she was equally certain she was about to join her in the hereafter. Especially when the kids all began to walk toward the base of the platform, lowering their torches.

There was a wooshing noise, the updraft from the fire was instantaneous. Heat licked the soles of her feet, and the metal pole began to warm. She struggled against her bonds, shaking the man in front of her, wrenching her wrist around and hearing the bones in his hand crack before he groaned, pained and weak. He was going to be no help.

The flames were getting higher, the metal pole nearly hot enough to burn, and the smoke was thick. She pressed her face into the flannel shirt of the man in front of her, breathing deep the scent of blood and sweat, but getting a lung full of clean, smokeless air before she finally began to scream.

*The train stopped. The door swung open. The man stood and stepped to the threshold, looking out at the world. It was night, the air was chilled, but not uncomfortable. The tracks were on top of a hill, overlooking a small town. Nearby there were a couple of warehouses, empty and abandoned as the last trains to use these tracks had long since been decommissioned. A river ran through the town and appeared to spill out into a giant body of water that stretched out far past his vision. The man took a deep breath through his nose, hoping to catch the salt air of the ocean, but instead, he caught the acrid scent of woodsmoke and burning and it reminded him that he wanted a cigarette.*

*He stepped off the train and the door closed behind him before the giant beast began moving again, quiet now that he was on the outside. He reveled in that peace as he started his walk toward town, but then a scream broke that silence. He closed his eyes, standing stock still as the sound died away. He stood there a minute more, barely breathing before it came again, broken this time, but close by. "God-fucking-damnit," he muttered before he took off at a run in the direction of the screams.*

Detective Cole sidestepped a pool of blood and skirted around the EMTs that hovered over the very dead woman in the doorway. There had been a trail of blood leading away from the apartment, stopping at the road. Either one of the attackers had been injured, or there was a second victim. The bleeding person had been taken to the street and likely put into a vehicle. Just like this morning, Cole thought, surveying the rest of the crime scene. There didn't seem to be much of a struggle past the doorway. It was a simple apartment, an open layout for the kitchen and living/dining room. A computer desk with a bulky Compaq tower and monitor sat in the corner of the living room, screensaver flashing. A hall led to three doors, he assumed two bedrooms and a bath. One of the doors was open, and he caught sight of two green eyes peering at him from a few inches above the ground. The cat scurried back into the bedroom when he walked toward it. He shut the door to make sure the animal did not escape while they were investigating.

It was when he was walking back into the kitchen that he noticed the camera bag on the kitchen island. His eyes narrowed and he grabbed it, reaching into the front pocket and pulling out his business card. He cursed under his breath.

The static squelch of the radio broke through his thoughts. "Smoke sighted out at the Mechanic Street complex," said dispatch.

Someone at the fire station replied, "We're sending a truck."

Cole opened his mouth before he had a chance to second-guess his words. "Get an ambulance out there," he said to the closest EMT.

The medic looked at him, frowning. "They haven't called for-"

Cole sighed and took the radio from the man's shoulder, pushing the button. "This is Detective Jonathan Cole, I need an ambulance out at the Mechanic Street complex ASAP." He replaced the radio in its clip, patting the EMT on the arm and saying, "Thank you," as he rushed out the door.

Julia couldn't scream anymore, the smoke filled her lungs and threatened what was left of her clear-headedness. Despite the weakness, she felt like she was beginning to make some headway against the ropes. The heat was making her sweat, making the bonds around her hands and wrists slick and slightly more workable. The black-eyed kids had all stepped away from the flames, retreating to the far corners of what she could now see was a giant, empty warehouse. None of them came forward when she got her first hand free and began working at the ropes on the other hand. Her co-captive, nothing more than dead weight against her and the pole, had passed out completely from smoke inhalation. She wriggled, shimmying down and wincing as her cheek touched the hot metal, but moments later she was free of the ropes around her torso. With less restricted movement, she was able to get her free arm over to release the other hand from the nearly-dead man, then begin the work on the ropes around her waist.

Out of the corner of her eye, through thickening smoke, she saw a flash of movement. Squinting, she saw one of the hooded kids lying on the ground near an open door. Another flash and two more bodies were crumpled to the ground ten feet from the first. A tall, lean young man stood over them. He cast a glance up at her, then turned to face a group of four kids that were heading his way. He easily dodged the first attacker, grabbing his wrist and wrestling a knife from his hand. He brandished it at the other three, and they all hesitated before turning and running for the closest door. He spun around, and realizing there were no more attackers, he approached the pyre and tossed the knife up to Julia.

She missed the catch, but it buried itself in the platform at her feet, and she was able to pull it loose without issue. A moment later, she was free. The flames were licking around the edges of the platform now, sneaking up through knots in the wood. She coughed, hard enough to see spots before steadying herself and turning to the man still attached to the pole. Was he even breathing?

"He's not dead," the young man said from his spot a few feet from the fire. "Not yet at least - but you might want to hurry if you want to play hero. You're running short on time."

Julia got to work, slicing quickly through the ropes. The stranger was working to clear a spot near the platform enough for Julia and the nearly-dead man to get down without burning to death. She could hear him cussing above the crackling flames. When the last rope was cut, the man, the old woman had called him "Little Timothy" she finally remembered, fell hard to the platform, shaking it and causing sparks to fly up around them in the updraft. The stranger reached for him, grabbing a handful of flannel and yanking him toward the edge of the platform and over it. Julia heard a thud as he hit the ground. A few seconds later the stranger's face appeared at the edge of the platform. "Need me to catch ya?"

She doubled over in a coughing fit, and the stranger grabbed her sleeve, using her misplaced center of gravity to topple her off the platform and onto his shoulder. Upside down, her lungs protested further and she found herself coughing into the waistband of his jeans before he tossed her unceremoniously to the dusty ground next to Nearly-Dead Little Timothy. They were still a little too close to the fire, and the stranger took one of Tim's hands, nodding to Julia to take the other. Together they dragged the unconscious man to the far wall near an open door.

Julia gasped in the fresh air, as consciousness threatened to recede. The stranger peeked out into the darkness beyond, nodding after a moment before he returned to Timothy. Julia watched him, dazed and perplexed, as he began searching Timothy's pockets. "Bingo," he grinned, pulling a pack of cigarettes from the man's shirt. He popped one in his mouth, then shoved his hand in his own pocket, pulling out a zippo. He flipped it open, flicking the wheel but got nothing. "Damnit," he said, and turned his back to her. "This town have any cops?" he asked as he searched the edges of the fire. He found the end of a stick and pulled it from the pyre, using the lit end to light his cigarette before he tossed it back into the flames. He took a long, savoring drag before turning back to her. "Because you might want to call them."

# CHAPTER FOUR

She was in the back of the ambulance when Cole arrived at the scene, sitting on the bumper, wrapped in a blanket. Her face was dusted with ash, and there was a bandage on her right cheek. She held a bottle of water with one hand, and an oxygen mask in the other. She was staring at the warehouse, the smoke puffing out of the long broken windows, in a daze until Cole crossed her field of vision. She blinked and offered him a weak smile as he walked over.

"I have to tell you, Miss Winters," he said, pulling out his notepad, "this is a whole new level of being somewhere you shouldn't be."

She laughed, but choked on it and began to cough. He took the hand with the oxygen mask in his, guiding it up to cover her nose and mouth. She nodded her thanks to him. "Sorry," she said after the coughing fit subsided.

"You're fine," he said, then frowned. "Has anyone spoken to you about Tabitha Browning?"

She looked up at him and he noticed that there were muddy streaks in the ash on her face. "She's dead, isn't she? They killed her…" her voice trailed off.

"Can you tell me who did this, Miss Winters?" he asked. "I know you've been through a lot tonight, but if there's anything you can tell me, maybe we can get who did this to you."

Julia's gaze searched the scene again. The fire crews were finishing up in the warehouse. The other ambulance had left as Cole arrived, taking Tim Knox to the hospital for a critical care reunion with his father. She looked like she was searching for something, but then she shrugged. "I'm hungry," she said as she brought her eyes back to him. "Can we get some food?"

Cole blinked, "Some food? Yeah, sure." He put his notepad back into his pocket. "Let me make sure the medic has cleared you, then I'll take you to Syd's Diner."

She nodded. "Feed me waffles and I'll tell you everything I know, Detective."

The man from the train had made himself scarce as soon as he heard the sirens. He'd stuck around for a little bit, out of sight, just to make sure the little black-eyed bastards didn't return before there were enough rescue workers there to fight them off. When he saw that the girl was getting bandaged up, he took off toward town. He had pondered, briefly, setting up in one of the abandoned warehouses, but the idea of a hot shower and a soft bed, something he hadn't really had in more years than he cared to count, was too enticing. He reached into his pocket, pulling out the pack of cigarettes and the wallet he'd palmed from the unconscious guy. He pulled the cash from it, then tossed the rest into a big blue mailbox as he passed by the first real buildings into town. A couple hundred bucks and some smokes wasn't a lot to ask in payment for a heroic rescue, was it?

~ ~ ~

Syd's Diner was nearly empty at this hour on a weekday, which was a blessing as Julia had become acutely aware of how she must look. Singed and bandaged, reeking of woodsmoke and worse. Cole's disheveled air of sleeplessness looked positively polished next to her, but the waitress didn't bat an eye and before long their food was served. Her throat burned, but that didn't stop her from shoveling a full order of waffles, plus bacon, into her mouth the second it hit the table.

Detective Cole waited patiently, sipping a cup of black coffee and poking at a mixture of scrambled eggs and hash browns that he had coated in hot sauce. "Do you have a place you can go tonight?" he asked.

Julia looked up, swallowing a huge bite of waffle. "I'm honestly not sure." She looked at the clock above the door, it read 12:15. The way she'd left Devin, she imagined he would be dead to the world until well after sunrise.

"The Lake Hotel isn't busy this time of year, I can get you set up with a room for the night if you like." Cole paused. "You should also know I'm going to have an officer checking in on you for the next few days."

Julia frowned. "Is that necessary?"

"Miss Win-"

"Julia," she interrupted. "If you're going to assign me a stalker, at least use my first name."

Cole sighed. "Julia. Yes, it's necessary. You were kidnapped by someone who has yet to be caught. There's no guarantee they won't try to take you again. You are getting a stalker."

Julia frowned. "Fine," she said around a piece of bacon. Then after a moment, she said, "Thank you."

Cole nodded. "So. Did you see who took you?"

A chill crept up Julia's spine. "Yes. There were two of

them at the door. They followed me home from Devin's apartment."

Cole had pulled out his notebook. "Do you have descriptions?"

"Teenagers, maybe. No older. Wearing dark hooded sweatshirts." She paused, feeling her throat close as the memories she'd been keeping at bay began closing in. "They had black eyes."

Cole looked up. "Like, they were on drugs or something? Blown out pupils?"

Julia closed her eyes, the chill blossoming into a shudder. "No. Fully black, no whites at all."

A crease formed between Cole's eyebrows. "That's what Mr. Knox meant, then. How strange…"

"There were more of them at the warehouse when I came to," Julia continued. "I would guess eight, maybe more. All kids, all black eyes."

"How did you escape eight murderous teenagers?"

"There was a man," Julia said. "He came out of nowhere, started taking them out. The rest of them ran. I guess the few he'd knocked out woke up and snuck out before the fire trucks came. I didn't see them, they just disappeared. So did the guy who saved us."

"What did the guy look like? Did he have black eyes too?"

"No. Just a normal guy, I guess. Tall, shaggy brown hair. Kind of dirty and beat up honestly, and he stole Little Timothy's cigarettes."

"Could just be some transient that happened by," Cole said. "You got lucky."

Julia nodded.

"So, you talked about these kids with black eyes at the hospital. You were curious about them…"

Julia averted her eyes, looking down at her empty plate.

"Anything you can tell me will only help to stop this," Cole said.

"You're going to think I'm crazy Detective Cole," she said before looking up and meeting his gaze.

"Try me," he smiled.

She took a breath and then dove in. "When I was young, my family had a run in with black-eyed kids. We were at a truck stop in the middle of nowhere, and these two kids knocked on the driver's window, wanting a ride. My dad, he was such a good guy, he opened the door."

Cole's smile had faded, but he was watching her intently.

"They killed my dad instantly," her stomach started churning and she began to regret the waffles. "My brother and I were in the back seat. He shoved me out of the car and tried to fight them off, but it was no use. We tried to run, but they were faster. Eventually, he pushed me on ahead to flag down a truck, and he turned to fight, to buy me time. By the time I got to safety and turned around, they were gone, just disappeared like ghosts. The only thing left was the car... and my dad."

"I'm so sorry, Julia," Cole said.

"I'd almost started to believe I'd imagined it somehow, you know? Like the shrink my aunt made me see when I was young was right, and that I'd made up some horrible monster to replace the memory of something worse." She looked up, meeting Cole's eyes. "But, when I got older, I started looking into it, and these things have been seen all over the world. There are sightings of them all throughout the 20th century. And I didn't imagine it tonight."

Cole was watching her closely, face unreadable. At least he wasn't laughing, or worse, looking at her with that pity that comes when someone had written her off as insane. "What did the police say?"

Julia shook her head. "Nothing of use." She took a sip of water, coughing slightly. "They never found the killers, and they never found Gene." She paused, fiddling with the cracked Formica under her empty plate. "I never found Gene..."

Cole flipped the page on his notepad. "Where did this happen? What was your father's name?"

Julia blinked, "This little diner in the middle of nowhere in the mountains, west of Grand Junction. It's been demolished since then," she said. "Dad's name was Charles Winters."

Cole scratched the info onto his paper. "It could be connected, Julia - you never know." He looked up, reaching forward and putting a warm hand on her arm. "If there's more evidence to be found, anything that could help you find out what happened to your brother, I'll find it."

Tears welled in her eyes. "You believe me?"

Cole squeezed her arm and drew his hand back. "While I'm not quite ready to believe in homicidal ghost teens," he said and stood up, "I'm currently estimating your possible insanity at only fifty percent if that helps."

She wiped her eyes and laughed. "Thanks a lot, Detective Cole," she said.

He helped her out of the booth, leading her toward the door. "Anytime, Miss Winters."


*"They got away,"* the voice was low, a wind-eroded gravestone.

The man flinched at the pain it caused in his head, clutching the steering wheel. "I know. I'm sorry." In the distance, the smoke from the warehouse was dissipating into the sky, the fire completely out.

*"You said you could do it,"* said the other voice, lighter, more feminine, a monotone whine.

"I know, I will."

*"You promised you would get us home,"* said the first.

*"We trusted you,"* said the second.

"I will do it. You can trust me." A tear slipped down the man's cheek and he brushed at it angrily before he turned the car around and headed back toward town.

Julia stepped out of the shower at the hotel and glared at her dirty, smoke-filled clothes. There were blood stains on the collar of her white button-up shirt, and she promised herself she would buy a replacement in the morning. She pulled on the jeans, the worst that had happened to them was smoke damage, and pulled her black camisole over her head. The dampness of her skin set aloft a whole new range of smells from the fabric, but she didn't care. The hotel bar would be having last call within the next half hour, and she was certain she wasn't getting to sleep tonight without at least one shot of whiskey. She glanced in the mirror. The bandage gone from her cheek, there was an ugly red mark where she'd been burned, but it didn't appear to be blistering. There were dark circles under her eyes, unsurprisingly. She stuck her tongue out at herself before she left the room.

The motel itself was nearly eighty years old, built as a riverside resort, it had been revamped and updated unevenly throughout the decades. The carpeting was a deep, dark red, presumably replaced in the seventies, but the wallpaper had been "restored" to the 1920's art deco of its former glory. Dark, heavy wood trim was in dire need of conditioning, and the smell of ancient cigar smoke clung to every surface in varying degrees. The hallways and stairwells were empty on her way to the bar. Visions of Stephen King stories danced in her head with every corner she turned, but soon the unfortunate sounds of late night karaoke broke through the silence, and she followed it across the lobby to her destination.

There were half a dozen people sitting at tables around a makeshift stage watching a woman prance stumblingly to a Madonna song. She turned away from the scene and found a seat at one of the mismatched bar stools. "A pint of whatever's on tap," she said to the bartender. "And a shot of Jameson, please." The bartender nodded, placing her drinks in front of her and taking the cash she laid on the bar. She downed the shot first, gesturing for another before settling in and taking a sip of the beer.

"Rough day, huh?" a voice from a few seats away.

Julia rolled her eyes, turning to look at the voice's owner, a snarky remark poised on her tongue, but it died in her throat when she recognized him as the stranger from the warehouse. He looked like he'd taken a shower, his hair was damp and he looked cleaner, though he still wore the same stained t-shirt and jeans. It was hard to tell in the dim light, but he looked like he had been in a fight before tonight. An older bruise on the side of his face, and maybe the darkness under his right eye was not just from lack of sleep.

He moved over a few chairs, leaving one empty between them. He brought a glass with him, a tumbler full of amber liquid and ice. "Glad to see you're up and around."

"Yeah," Julia stumbled. "I mean, thank you." She turned to face him. "I mean… you saved my life tonight."

He shrugged, taking a sip of his drink, "You caught me on a good day." He turned his full attention to her. "I'm Bash," he offered his hand and she took it, feeling rough calluses on his palm. "And you are…?"

Julia flushed, "Sorry, I'm Julia. Julia Winters."

Bash took his hand back, wrapping it around the

tumbler, drawing a pattern in the condensation with his thumb. "Julia Winters, huh?" He said slowly, then he smirked, shaking his head. "That is interesting."

She frowned. "What?"

"Not a thing," he said. He tilted back the drink, finishing it. "Nice to meet you, Winters." He stood from his barstool, tipping a hat that he didn't have, and turned on his heel, leaving her behind to order another shot.

# CHAPTER FIVE

The man from the train... the transient hero... the frustrated insomniac.

Bash was on his back, arms folded under his head, on the most comfortable bed he'd had the pleasure of encountering in as long as he could remember, and he could not sleep. The red numbers floating in the dark above the bedside table told him it was after four in the morning. The train had taken him far from where he had come... So how is it that those black-eyed bastards were here, too?

His heart had stopped when he saw how many there were in the warehouse. Where he'd come from, two of them could take down a group of ten without batting a soulless, pitch-dark eye. He had almost turned and walked back out, but one of them caught sight of him and attacked. Instinctively he had blocked the knife coming into his left side and swung with a wide right hook. He heard a pained gasp as he connected with the creature's jaw, and he swung again, knocking him to the ground. At the time, he didn't think about it. He'd taken down two others before he noticed the blond girl struggling against her bonds. By the time he'd helped her, the rest of the kids were gone.

Now he was starting to wonder about his luck. Those sons of bitches never went down easy. He'd personally witnessed their resilience on many occasion. He had watched one that had been impaled pull rebar free of her gut and use it to kill one of his crew. He had seen one practically bisected by a machete advance on a group of people, killing all within reach, until the last threads of muscle and viscera had given out and its spine had snapped under the weight of its dangling torso. How in the hell had he survived nearly a dozen of them?

*And Julia Winters? Seriously?* He chuckled ruefully, flipping over onto his stomach. *In a universe of infinite possibility…*

Julia woke to a knock on the door. She groaned, feeling everything her body had been through in the last eighteen hours hit her like a speeding train.

"Miss Winters? You okay in there?" Cole's voice on the other side of the door.

Julia groaned again, tempted to hide her head under the soft hotel pillows.

"Julia if you don't give me a response with some kind of human language, I'm going to have to kick the door in."

Julia whined and pushed herself out of bed, slouching heavy-footed to the thin door and throwing it open, scowling.

Detective Cole smiled broadly at her, holding a coffee and a bag of what smelled like donuts in one hand, and her purse and an overnight bag in the other. "Good morning, Miss Winters." He flushed slightly and turned his eyes to the upper door frame when he realized she

was dressed only in her underwear and camisole. "I uh…
I didn't think you had any of your clothes with you, and
um… you can't get back into your apartment for at least
another twenty-four hours, so I picked up some of your
stuff for you."

Julia's own embarrassment flashed for a moment until
she processed his words. "At least twenty-four hours?"
She took the overnight bag from him and headed toward
the bathroom door. "But what about my cat?"

Cole came into her room, placing the rest of his
armload onto the small breakfast table in the middle of
the room. "I fed him and watered him," Cole said to the
closed bathroom door. "I moved his litter into a
bedroom with him - to make sure he doesn't escape
when the cleaners come in."

Julia opened the bathroom door, sticking her head
out. "Really? You did?"

"Yeah," Cole said. "You know, your cat is kind of an
asshole."

Julia laughed, leaving the door open a crack while she
finished pulling on clean pants and a shirt. "He has
discerning taste." She checked herself in the mirror.
Clean clothes did wonders for her mood. She leaned into
the mirror, seeing that the red mark on her cheek was
covered in tight, dry skin now. She flexed her jaw, testing
the pain and found it manageable. When she came back
into the room proper, Cole was sitting on the edge of her
unmade bed, studying what appeared to be a series of
tiny scratches on the back of his right hand. "Oh no, I'm
sorry," she said, going to him to have a closer look. "He
really is an asshole. I might have some band-aids in my
bag."

"It's fine, really," Cole laughed, standing. "I'm sure
I've suffered worse in the line of duty."

Julia was searching through her bag for the band-aids

and saw her pager light up. The buzzing vibrating off a small change pocket in the side of the bag.

"That happened about six times on the way over here," Cole said.

Julia picked it up and scrolled through. Devin's number, nine times, each time with another "911" added to the end. "Did Tabitha's murder make it to the news this morning?"

Cole nodded, "Oh yes. It's a small town, Julia. Everyone is talking about the murder and the warehouse fire."

Julia sighed and put the pager back in her bag. "Can I bother you for a ride to the Photo Shack?"

Bash had been staring at the front page of the newspaper for five minutes when he heard the Winters girl and her companion coming down the hall toward the lobby. The overstuffed armchair he'd been sitting in was facing the big picture window at the front of the hotel, away from the hallway. He sank into the chair, opening the paper in front of him while they passed. Once they were outside, he lowered the paper and watched them walk past the window. She had found clean clothes, something he needed to procure sooner than later. The man with her, obviously a cop, opened the passenger side door of a Buick to let her in. *Very gentlemanly,* Bash thought with a cocked brow.

"Did you want any more coffee?" a voice broke Bash's focus. A pretty dark-haired girl was standing at the counter where breakfast had been offered to hotel guests. She turned, smiling at him. "I can make some more if you want." She blushed. "I mean, we're not supposed to after 10, but I won't tell if you don't."

Bash offered her one of his more charming smiles, "Darlin', I would love some more coffee," he said, sitting up straight in his chair and downing the rest of what was in his cup. "And maybe, if you've got any extra, another one of those frosted apple things."

"A danish?" she asked.

"That's the thing, doll," he said.

She hesitated, then smiled. "I'll get you one, just give me a second."

When she left the room, Bash stood and stretched, then folded the newspaper and shoved it in his back pocket without looking at the date again. He would delve into that whole issue later, there were more important things to be dealt with first.

The brunette came back in with a half pot of fresh coffee and an apple danish wrapped in cellophane. "Here," she said, handing it to him with a lingering look at his face. "Is there anything else I can get you?"

Bash smirked, "As a matter of fact, yes, there is."

Devin was tall, an easy six foot five, with the reach of one who could slam dunk a basketball without much effort, so when he greeted Julia by wrapping his arms around her in a panicked hug, she felt very much like she was being lovingly attacked by an octopus. After a long moment, he pulled back, studying her face, touching her cheek below the burn mark, then pulled her in for another hug, kissing her on top of her head.

Cole coughed.

Devin let her go and they turned to see the detective rifling through a stack of photo paper.

"Is this Officer Dishy?" Devin said, shaking off the affection and leaning back against the counter.

Cole turned around, brows furrowed.

"Detective," Julia said.

Devin smiled lazily, eyeing the disheveled detective. "Detective Dishy. I like that better."

Julia hid her own smile as she watched a blush creep up Cole's cheeks.

"Cole, this is Devin," Julia introduced. "Devin this is Detective Cole. Be nice to him."

Devin shook Cole's hand. "Nice to meet you. You're very photogenic."

Julia stomped on his foot and changed the subject hastily when Cole raised an eyebrow at her. "I forgot to tell you, I saw the guy at the hotel last night."

Cole's second eyebrow joined the first near his hairline. "The guy?"

"The guy, the transient guy that saved us!"

"Oh!" Cole said, pulling his notepad from his pocket. "That guy! Did you talk to him?"

"Yeah," Julia said, frowning. "A little. He was odd. Said his name was Bash."

Cole looked like he was about to ask another question when his phone rang. "Sorry, I'll be right back," he said and went out the door.

Julia turned back to Devin and found herself wrapped up again in one of his overwhelming hugs. "I'm so glad you're okay, Jules."

The sincerity in his voice caught her off guard, and she felt the heaviness of the last day collect in a lump in her throat and a stinging pressure behind her eyes. A laugh, thick with tears escaped her mouth. "Me too."

Bash was exhausted. He had asked the pretty brunette, *Is her name Maggie? Meg? Hell, I don't know...* to point him in the direction of a store where he could get some inexpensive clothing. She had insisted on taking him herself since her shift was nearly up, and now he found himself standing in Grand River Resale, arms full of button-ups, ratty cardigans, and jeans that looked just as good as the torn and stained ones he was already wearing. It was either lack of sleep or the fact that the girl was nearly insufferable in her enthusiasm for clothes that was making him grind his teeth and curse her name, whatever it was, every time she turned away.

"Here," she said layering one more outfit atop the growing pile, "wear these together - they only work as an outfit, I think."

She smiled up at him, and he loosened his jaw and gave her a smile back. "Thanks, doll." He headed toward the register, vowing to throw away half of what she'd given him, but too tired and ready to be alone to argue. The total cost was twenty-five dollars, and he pulled forty from his pocket absently wondering where the next cash influx was going to come from. The room had cost more than he was expecting, but the date on the paper and more than a few decades worth of inflation had explained that. The "reward" he had procured was dwindling fast and he would have to figure something out soon.

"Do you have a place to go tonight?" the girl asked as they exited the store, bags in hand.

"I do not," he said and opened the driver's side door for her. "I was hoping to stay at your hotel another night, but I'm finding myself direly lacking in funds." He came around the other side of the car, settling into the passenger seat.

She gave him another too-enthusiastic smile. "I can get you a room! I've got a week's worth of free nights built up. You can use a day or two, for sure!"

*There it is,* thought Bash. Aloud he said, "I couldn't take those from you, darlin'."

"It's no problem at all, really!" she said. "We're not booked up this time of year anyway, and I don't really have any use for them at the moment."

"You're the greatest, kid," he said patting her on the

knee. He watched the blush creep up her cheeks. *If only they were all that easy...*

Detective Cole stood in the hall of the ICU where he had caught Julia trying to sneak into Mr. Knox's room less than twenty-four hours before. *Damn, it's been a long day,* he sighed, scribbling in his notebook. Both Timothy and his father had regained consciousness, and it was likely that they would be moved out of the ICU within the next couple of days. His father didn't remember much from the attack, so now that Tim was awake, Cole was hoping to get something substantial from the younger Knox.

"You can go in and see him now," a nurse said, kicking the door stop down to hold the room door open.

Timothy looked like hell. The right side of his face was covered in bandages, and his left eye was black and swollen. He introduced himself and showed his badge.

"Sorry to bother you, Mr. Knox. I just have a few questions, if you're up for it."

Timothy nodded, then winced.

"Do you remember what happened?"

"Yeah. Sort of." His words were slightly slurred with the pain medication, but understandable. "I was asleep on the couch, I'd been out late the night before and I didn't want to wake Dad up. The stairs are really squeaky." He made a sound in his throat, something similar to a rat or a mouse. Cole blinked and waited for him to continue. "I kind of heard the doorbell, but I was really conked out. I didn't really wake up until I heard Dad scream. Then I sat up and looked behind the couch and these three kids - I mean, they weren't kids, not like kindergarteners or anything. But like, kids - teenagers I guess. And they were hovering over my dad and..." Tim swallowed heavily. "There was so much blood."

"Take your time, Mr. Knox."

He nodded again. "And I yelled - I don't know what I yelled - I just yelled because Dad was so scared, you know? I could see it in his face. And then the kids turned around and-" Tim's color drained, the pallid white splotches contrasting sickeningly with the dark bruises. "Their eyes were completely black."

*Yes, I know. I've heard it and I don't have any answers for you - please just continue.* Cole searched his brain for a more appropriate, comforting response and came up empty.

Tim took a breath and continued. "They um, they came at me and one of them bashed me on the head with something. Mostly everything is a blur after that. I just remember little snippets until waking up here."

"Anything at all that you remember may be useful, Mr. Knox."

Tim frowned. "They didn't say much if anything at all. I just remember being carried. I kind of remember being in a car. Then I was in and out of consciousness when they were tying me to a pole. Was I tied to a pole?"

Cole nodded. "Yes. You and another victim were tied to a support beam in an abandoned warehouse. She was able to get you both loose."

"The blond girl?" Tim asked. "That was real?"

Cole smiled. "Yes."

"Huh," Tim said. "I should probably get her flowers or something."

Cole laughed. "Is there anything else you remember? Anyone talking at all?"

"Just once. Someone older maybe? It could have been a dream, but it sounded like he was giving instruction to them."

Cole perked up. "An older man? Do you remember anything else?"

Tim shook his head. "I'm sorry. It's all so jumbled." He made a motion with his hands that looked like drunken juggling.

Cole pulled a business card from his pocket. "That's ok, Mr. Knox, I understand. Please call me if you remember anything else, okay?" Tim nodded and Cole left, making a few more notes as he walked. It was only a small thing, but some adult pulling the strings on these kids was the first thing that made much sense in the last thirty-six hours.

# CHAPTER SIX

Bash slid the keycard through the slot on his hotel room door. The light flashed red. He did it again with the same result. The night before, after he checked in, he'd stared at the plastic card with trepidation for a full thirty seconds before someone happened by and took pity, assuming he'd been drinking. He had watched them closely, assuming that he had it figured out, until now.

"Let me help."

Bash gritted his teeth, handing the card to the peppy brunette. "Sure, thanks."

"Yeah," she said, sliding it through and getting a green light. "These are still pretty new here. Sometimes they can be a little touchy." She swung the door open and let herself in.

Bash closed his eyes and prayed for patience. His exhaustion was finally at the level where he thought he just might get some sleep, providing he could get rid of his helpful little tagalong.

"You really don't have anything, do you?" she asked, looking around at the lack of bags and personal items. "I can get you some free stuff from the front desk tonight. Toothbrush and toothpaste, a comb, a razor if you want, but we don't have any shaving cream."

"You're too good to me, doll," he said. He stood to the side of the door, propping it open with his foot, his arms still laden with the bags from the clothing store. "Now. I'm sure you're tired, after an all-night shift, then taking care of me all morning."

She came over and took his bags, tossing them to the side on the floor. "No, I don't go to bed until late afternoon." She smiled up at him. "I've got hours before then."

Bash took a breath and opened his mouth to say something, but was thwarted when she lifted herself up on her tiptoes and kissed him. Not a chaste, nice-to-meet-you, maybe-we-can-get-dinner kind of kiss, but more of a you're-not-getting-sleep-anytime-soon kind of kiss. She had maneuvered the door closed, and he was pushed back against it, the doorknob digging into his hip. He quickly calculated the repercussions of letting this scenario play itself out, and put his hands on her shoulders, gently pushing her back. "Whoa, sweetheart," he said. "I'm an old-fashioned kinda guy. A toothbrush and a razor isn't enough to get into these dusty trousers."

She looked up at him, confused. "Seriously?"

He snaked his arm around behind him, opening the door and sliding her through it. "Serious as a heart attack, doll." He leaned down and kissed her on the cheek. "Thanks for everything, though. You're the best."

Her confused expression didn't change as he shut the door on her. To be on the safe side, he slid the chain lock into place before he stumbled forward, falling face first onto the freshly made bed. He was going to need a lot more rest before he was ready to tackle this world.

~ ~ ~

"I saw them kids."

Julia jumped, spinning around to face the alley next to the Photo Shack. Devin came down the step behind her, putting a hand on her shoulder. "Jesus, Jerry," he said.

"I'm sorry," the old man said, shifting to hide within his raggedy clothes a little better. His eyes darted from Julia and Devin to the street a few blocks down where a police car was swinging by on patrol. "I just wanted your friend to know - I'm glad she's ok." He raised his voice slightly, as though Julia was standing across the street instead of a few feet away. "I'm glad you're okay. I saw them kids that night. They were waiting out here for you."

Julia felt her arms and cheeks go numb. "What?"

"Them kids without the eyes. They were here. Scariest thing I ever saw," his voice dropped to a whisper. "I'm just glad you're okay. You be careful." He nestled down further, disappearing altogether as the police car stopped in the street next to them and the uniformed officer in the driver's seat rolled her window down.

"Miss Winters?" Julia nodded and the officer continued. "I'm Sargent Biggs. Detective Cole wanted me to swing by and check on you."

"Awwwwww," Devin said under his breath, threading his arm through hers. "Detective Dishy is checking up on you."

"That's enough," she muttered, turning to smile at policewoman. "Thank you. I was just heading back to the hotel. Probably stay there for the rest of the night."

Biggs returned her smile. "That's a good plan, Miss Winters. Let us know if you need anything, okay?" Julia nodded, and the officer waved before letting the cruiser inch forward down the road.

When the car was out of sight, Julia looked up at

Devin, the old man's words swimming in her skull. "Would you stay with me tonight?"

He frowned. "Hmmm, a nice hotel or a crummy apartment…"

"There's karaoke at the bar."

"Hotel it is," he said and swept her into the front seat of her car. "You sure know how to tempt a man, Jules."

Detective Cole coughed, the acrid scent of watered down charred wood infiltrating his throat and lungs. The warehouse was still standing, but the damage inside was enough to condemn the place. The early afternoon sun shone through the high windows highlighting the excessive smoke dust still in the air but didn't cast much light on to the floor where he stood. He reached into his pocket and pulled out a small flashlight, the beam was wide, but dim in the haze.

The minimal police force in Grand River had combed the place, finding nothing. Cole was convinced they'd missed something, but it wasn't until he went back over his notes from his first interview with Julia that it clicked. He swung the beam to the center of the room, it dusted over what was left of the pyre. Burnt wood piled four feet high in places, fifteen feet across. There was every likelihood that the cops had not scoured the rubble thoroughly. He nudged the log closest to him, kicking up ash and dust that danced in the beam of his flashlight. With a sigh, he pulled his sleeve over his hand, placed it over his nose and mouth, and trudged into the mess.

A half an hour later, he grinned in triumph and pulled a plastic glove and evidence bag out of his pocket. The knife that Julia had used to cut herself free was mostly intact. It was just a kitchen knife, really. The wooden handle had been slightly charred, but not wholly. Hopefully there was enough left to pull a print or two.

He was almost back to his car when his phone rang.

"Hey Cole." It was Sergeant Biggs "We found the Knox boy's wallet. Post worker brought it in after finding it in the mailbox on Maple Ave. You want me to run prints on it."

"Hell yes, I do," he said, "and I have a weapon from the scene that I'm bringing in for prints as well."

Biggs laughed. "Overachiever," she said before the disconnecting click.

Cole sat in his car and rested his hands on the wheel, breathing a sigh of clean air and relief. Weapons, wallets, and prints were all tangible things. This case would be cracked just like every other case, demon children be damned.

Bash slept that afternoon, but he slept restlessly. Memories haunted his dreams. A young man with shaggy hair, scared and alone. *I can't get you home and I can't keep you alive. The good news, you can keep yourself alive and I'll show you how. But you're going to have to pull your weight. I don't accept freeloaders.* Blood flowing down the boy's face, a knife wound from his brow to his cheek and through an eye that might never work again. That image morphed to the same face with many decades added onto it, the scar pinched and faded and barely noticeable past the expression of murderous hatred. A voice not his own plucked from memory, *This is what happens when a kid gets lucky on your watch. Don't you dare preach to me about guts. I may be an old man now, but there was a time where you were the adult, sending kids out with sticks and broken guns.* Bash felt the hands tighten around his neck, and bolted up in bed, gasping.

The floating red letters above his bedside table told him that it was 7:30 pm. A low beam of sunlight sliced through the small gap in his curtains, bisecting the room with dust moats. He focused on them, studying their dance while he let the memories flee back to the recesses of his mind where they belonged. He swiveled his head, running a hand back through his hair, over his stubble-covered cheeks, trying to brush away the feeling of fingers digging into his windpipe. The knock on the door pulled him further from his dreams and back to the world completely.

"Hi!" said the brunette desk clerk. She pushed past him and into his room, flipping on the light. "I brought you those things you asked for."

Bash closed his eyes. "But, I didn't actually ask-"

"No need to thank me," she smiled at him and began pulling the sheets and blanket back into their places on the bed, smoothing them while she talked. "I figured I'd bring them over before I started my shift."

"When does your shift start?"

"Nine o' clock!" She grabbed a small black box from the nightstand and sat on the end of the bed, patting the space next to her. "Want to catch some TV before I go in?" She lifted the little box and pointed it in front of her. The television screamed to life and she winced, lifting the box and pointing it again. The television slowly quieted to manageable noise.

Bash grimaced, "I wish I could but I've got someone I'm supposed to meet soon." He calculated every misstep he might take in giving her any wiggle room to stay longer.

"I thought you said you were just passing through town and didn't know anybody."

*Shit.* He pushed himself away from the door and sauntered toward her. Crouching down in front of where she sat on the bed, he took her hands in his and rested them on top of her knees. "I promise you that I will come visit you at the front desk tonight, sweetheart." He stood, lifting her hands gently so she had to stand with him, and led her back to the door. "Thanks again," he said and pushed her gently out into the hallway.

"Wait," she said, and he paused just before the door closed on her. "Are you meeting a girl?"

He blinked and shrugged, "I have no idea. Catch ya later, kid." The door closed before she could say anything else, and Bash again made sure the chain lock was in place before he grabbed the bag of supplies the girl had brought him and headed toward the shower.

On the floor above Bash, Julia was staring at the front page of the paper with disgust as Devin searched the empty drawers for treasure left behind and forgotten by the previous tenants.

"Looks like the maids are great at clearing the place, if not actually cleaning the place." He brought dusty fingers out of a cupboard and made a face, wiping them on the carpeting.

"Do you see this bullshit?" Julia asked, showing him the paper.

Devin took it, reading aloud, "Tribune Photographer Nearly Dies in Warehouse Fire." He looked up at her. "Is that not accurate?"

She grabbed it back from him, "I'm freelance, for one. Plus look at that photo!" She opened the paper again, pointing at a dark, blurred image. "This is what happens when you let novices take photos with these ridiculous new digital cameras."

Devin mouthed the word, "Oh," and nodded sympathetically before continuing his search, pulling the Bible from the nightstand and flipping through it upside down, shaking it.

"Her idiot son bought himself a digital camera and has been calling himself a photographer for the last few months," Julia huffed.

"Jules, you weren't really in a state to take the photo yourself," Devin said, frowning at the lack of money or love notes falling from the book.

"Yes, but she put this on the front page - which means to me that she doesn't see the difference between what's good and what's not - which means, I'm going to lose my best gig to a pretentious hack that's never touched a film canister in his life." Julia deflated, falling onto the bed next to Devin.

"She refers to you as a Tribune photographer on the front page - I think that indicates she's going to hold onto you for a while longer," he threw an arm around her shoulders, "at least as long as your nearly fatal evening keeps sales up."

Julia laughed a pained snort. "You're probably right." She flopped backward on the bed, staring up at the intricate molding on the ceiling. "It's been a long day, Devin."

He leaned back on his elbow, looking down at her. "Well, copious amounts of cheap booze and singing passionately to strangers will perk you right up." He bopped her on the nose gently with one long finger. "Now get up and get beautiful, my little peach tree. It's time we sing."

Cole's house was on the south end of downtown in a sprawling subdivision that had sprung up in the fifties to house the workers at the local paper mill. It was a small Craftsmen-style home in need of new paint, with a simple garden that he didn't take the time to tend. The porch light was off, per usual, allowing shadows to grow behind an unused porch swing.

He heard a sound behind him and turned to see two young people in hooded sweatshirts standing across the street, just out of the circle of light from the street lamp. His heart thumped against his chest and he held his breath, watching them. A long moment later, movement to his right drew his attention. A shadow darted out between his house and the next, across the street to meet the two hooded figures. It jumped on one of them, wrapping legs around its waist and pulling the hood down to reveal a smiling blond-haired boy. The shadow, now revealed in the light to be a slender teenage girl, giggled and kissed the boy. The third hooded figure groaned and mumbled something that Cole couldn't hear but assumed it was along the lines of, "Get a room." Cole shook his head, turning back to the door and unlocking it, making a mental note to tell his neighbor he might want to check for escape routes from his daughter's room.

The hallway he stepped into was dark as well, and his foot hit something soft and squishy that let out a slight "oof" when he kicked it again. "Get up, Stubbs," he said. "I'll get your food." The object at his feet huffed and jingled as it stood and moved toward the kitchen. Cole flipped on the light to reveal a what might have been a black lab if it weren't for a healthy dose of basset hound in his recent lineage. A long black body and wagging tail atop short, squatty legs, ears that dragged on the floor, and big, droopy eyes that looked up at Cole with expectation. "Want a treat?" Cole asked. The dog sat up on his hind legs, then leaned back farther, balancing on his tail so both sets of paws stood out in the air in front of him. Cole smiled and gave the dog a treat, then filled his bowl with food.

Cole's house was technically a three-bedroom home, with the master bedroom and a smaller bedroom on the first floor, and another bedroom taking up the entire second floor. The latter had been transformed into

Cole's office, however, and that's where he went now - walking past photos on the walls he had grown used to ignoring. He walked past the master bedroom, the door was closed and had been for five years - he was well adept at ignoring that, too.

The office wasn't messy, but it definitely had seen cleanlier times. Stacks of folders, envelopes, and papers were tucked away in corners and against furniture. There was a pillow and a blanket draped over the worn leather couch that served as Cole's bed on the rare occasion that he slept. Next to the couch was a mini fridge which he opened, taking out a bottle of light beer and a box of takeout Chinese. There was a laptop lying open and dark on his desk, and he ran his fingers along the keyboard to wake it up as he sat down in the worn but comfortable desk chair.

He was nearly done with the leftovers by the time the computer fully booted up and connected to the internet. He set it aside temporarily and opened up a browser window typing "Black-Eyed Kids" into his go-to search engine. He finished the rest of his food and got halfway through his beer while the engine searched for results. His eyes widened in disbelief as the results continued to populate, dozens upon dozens of pages dedicated to sightings. More pages discussing theory on who and what they were. He finished his beer and rolled his chair back to the fridge, pulling out another one. It was going to be a long night.

Bash looked at himself in the mirror. A shower and a shave, some new/used clothes and he felt almost human for the first time since he'd gotten on that train. Probably longer, if he was being honest. He wore loose fitting jeans that he'd belted around his waist and an untucked gray button-up over a plain t-shirt. He unbuttoned the cuffs on the dress shirt, folding them up to his elbows. He'd forgotten to find new shoes, but his old boots, though worn and dirty, were appropriate enough.

He pulled his pack of cigarettes from his shirt pocket and popped one in his mouth, taking a moment to admire his reflection as he lit it and inhaled deeply. *What the hell do I do now?* he thought to himself, then shrugged and after checking his pockets for that stupid plastic key, he left the room.

He was testing the key to ensure he could get back in his room when the elevator at the end of the hall opened and out stepped Julia Winters. She looked different, better, on a night where she hadn't been recently barbecued. Her silvery hair fell loose around her shoulders, and makeup accentuated large eyes and long dark lashes. Bash turned his attention to the man walking alongside her. He was tall and had an arm draped casually around the girl's shoulders.

Julia's glance slid over him, not seeing him. *Good,* he thought, but then his mouth opened and spoke before he could stop it. "Feeling better tonight, Winters?"

She stopped and turned, looking at him for a moment before it registered. "Oh!" she said. "It's you. I'm sorry, um, Bash, right?" She was flustered. A pink splotch appeared on her uninjured cheek.

He nodded, then held his hand out to the man next to her who was eyeing him with not a just a small amount of skepticism. "I'm Bash. Julia and I met last night."

The man took his hand, brows furrowed, "I'm Devin. By last night you mean...?"

"Crazy warehouse party," Bash said.

"This is the guy that helped me escape," Julia said. Her cheeks had almost returned to their normal color.

Devin's eyes widened. "You're the transient!" He frowned, looking Bash up and down. "Wait, *you're* the transient?"

Bash looked at Julia, watching the flush creep back to her face. "That's just what the cops thought- I mean- you were just- I mean you looked-" her hands came up in a gesture of surrender. "You clean up nice." Her face went pale and she put a hand to her mouth. "I mean-"

"Stop while you're ahead, Jules," Devin said.

Bash cocked an eyebrow thoughtfully. "In all honesty, 'transient' is a remarkable fit."

Julia looked up like she was about to apologize again, but Devin interrupted before she could dig herself deeper. "Well, Bash," he put a hand on Bash's shoulder, edging him away from the door and guiding him in the direction of the lobby. "You saved my best friend's life. The least we can do is buy you a drink."

Bash found himself ushered through the lobby. The brunette behind the front desk saw him and waved excitedly, he waved back and allowed Devin to lead him into the nearly empty barroom.

The bar retained some of the charm of the hotel's former glory. Dark wood with art deco embellishments. Thick crystal glassware hung in racks above the bar, and cigarette smoke hung heavy in the air. If the shrieking banshee currently singing on the stage were replaced with someone with a little more class and a lot more talent, with a better song, he might have felt as though he'd time-warped. Despite the music, he had found the place oddly comforting the night before and felt that comfort settle over him again as he sat at a high top near the bar with his new acquaintances.

"So," Devin said, nudging his stool closer to the small round table. "Where are you from, Bash?"

Bash pulled a thick crystal ashtray to the middle of the table. "All over, really," he said. Wordlessly he offered a cigarette to Julia, then Devin. Devin raised his eyebrows, reaching forward before Julia caught his glance. He lowered his hand and tried not to pout. Bash continued, "I've been traveling for as long as I can remember."

"Where did you come from last night?" Julia asked.

"I hopped off the train," he said. "As soon as I stepped off, I heard you scream."

"But," Julia's brows furrowed, "there aren't any trains on those tracks anymore. That particular line was there just for the warehouses, and they haven't operated in decades. I mean, those tracks are probably in gross disrepair and completely unusable by now."

"Huh." Bash flicked ash into the pristine ashtray. "Interesting."

Wilson Gardens was a neglected park about 10 blocks inland, away from the boardwalk and Jerry's usual stomping grounds at the Photo Shack. The rusting benches and dry fountain were occupied most nights, safety in numbers. Jerry had found a spot in the southeast corner, tucked in near a row of unkempt hedges that ran along a side street. He frowned, watching absently as a young woman hovered at an intersection. She fidgeted with her hair, smoothed her short shirt and adjusted her jacket.

Casting a glance up and down the street, Jerry didn't see anyone with her. It was dangerous for a girl to be turning tricks alone. She must be new. *Or maybe*, he thought with not much hope, *she is just waiting for a ride.*

The hooded kids seemed to come out of nowhere, two of them appearing behind her. She turned and started to say something, but the taller of the two hit her on the head with what looked like a small baton. Jerry shouted, drawing the attention of the kids as the young woman fell to the ground, coal black eyes zeroing in on him. Shouting for help, Jerry tried backing the chair through the break in the hedge, but his wheel stuck on a root.

Relief washed through him when a blue sedan came down the road, squealing tires at the intersection where the helpless girl lay. The back door opened and a man's voice yelled something that Jerry couldn't hear over his own shouts. The hooded kids stopped their pursuit of Jerry, turning their attention back to their original victim. Jerry's heart sank as they lifted her limp body and stuffed it into the back of the blue sedan before slipping into the back seat with her. By the time he thought to get the license plate, the car was already gone.

# CHAPTER SEVEN

The waitress came to take their orders. Bash ordered a gin and tonic, which seemed to please Devin as he ordered the same. Julia ordered a lager, watching Bash closely out of the corner of her eye and wondering what kind of question would be met with a straight answer, if any. She was about to dive in with her light interrogation when a woman with long dark hair and a bright smile came to their table.

"Who's singing tonight?" she asked, hefting a giant 3-ring binder onto the table between them. "Either of you boys interested in a duet?"

Bash looked at her quizzically. "Not a chance, sweetheart."

The woman smacked his arm playfully, "Oh, come on," she said. "You've got that sexy smoker's voice. I would bet you have a great singing voice."

Bash snuffed out his cigarette. "And you would be wrong."

"Maybe some Johnny Cash?" she suggested, flipping open the binder.

"I don't know who that is, lady," Bash said, annoyance creeping into his voice.

Devin took the binder from her. "I will be singing," he said. "Don't you worry."

The waitress brought their drinks, and the hostess drifted off to the next occupied table, slinging another big binder with her. Devin opened the book, then looked up at Bash. "You don't know who Johnny Cash is? Where have you been?" He grabbed a piece of paper and pencil from the front pocket of the binder, then began flipping pages.

Bash took a sip of his drink. "I've been away since the war."

Julia frowned. "The Gulf War?" Bash took another drink. "That was a decade ago - you don't look old enough to have been in the Gulf War."

Bash smirked. "Looks can be deceiving."

Again Julia opened her mouth to question him further, and again she was thwarted, this time by Devin.

"So Bash, are you just passing through town to somewhere else, or were you planning on staying for a while?"

Bash leaned back in his chair. "Most likely just passing through."

"That's too bad," Devin said, closing the book and sliding off his stool. "Jules needs a new roommate."

Julia's eyes opened wide. He was right, of course, but she wasn't about to invite some semi-transient drifter to live with her, no matter how much she owed him. She changed the subject quickly.

"So, do you have any family?" she asked. He was watching her, and she got the distinct impression that the reason for her subject change hadn't gone unnoticed.

He shook his head. "Nah. It was just my dad and me when I was young, but he's been gone a long time now."

He sipped his drink. "What about you?"

She shrugged. "Used to be Mom, Dad, Gene and me, now it's just me."

Bash shifted in his seat. "Gene?"

"Yeah" Julia nodded. "He's my brother. Disappeared a long time ago." She took a drink. "But anyway!"

"Anyway!" Devin said, swooping back into the conversation. "You kids are about to be witness to greatness. Shelby says I'm up after this warbling travesty." He gestured at the stage where a man was singing Jimmy Buffet with the passion of one that had probably listened to too much Jimmy Buffet in his lifetime. "Tough act to follow."

\*\*\*

# From the Message Boards

### Topic: Syracuse BEK Story

**Forgotten1968**  *7-13-1999, 4:53pm*
That lucky, lucky young lady.

**Raccoon**  *7-13-1999, 6:24pm*
The person who reported that story lost a friend, can you have some respect?

**Forgotten1968**  *7-13-1999, 6:30pm*
She's not lost, just in a different place.

**Raccoon**  *7-13-1999, 6:49pm*
Just stop.

\*\*\*

Bash stayed through Devin's song, expertly deflecting any further questioning from Julia. He congratulated

Devin on his performance, thanked them for the drink, and excused himself to the lobby. The brunette was behind the desk and she waved him over. He plastered on a smile, glancing at the name tag pinned to her vest. *Natalie? I wasn't even close.* "Good evening, Natalie," he said.

The girl frowned. "Natalie?" She looked down, pulling the vest forward to see the name tag. "Damn, I grabbed the wrong uniform." Then she looked up at him again, eyes narrowed. "What is my name?"

Bash widened his smile. "I didn't think that was right, but who am I to question a pretty girl's name tag?"

Her expression didn't change. Bash tempered his face to a more chagrined countenance and was about to plead his case, but the phone rang, rescuing him. She frowned and answered it, the anger on her face translated into her voice and he didn't envy the person on the other end of that call. He touched his fingers to his temple and bowed low, turning on his heel and walking out of the lobby before she had a chance to revoke his room for the night. He was not likely to get another night's stay out of her.

There was a man in the hallway near the door to Bash's room. He looked like he was talking to himself, gesturing angrily with one hand. When Bash got closer he could see that the man held a piece of brightly colored plastic to his ear. Bash could faintly hear another voice coming from the plastic, confirming his suspicion that it was some kind of phone. The man glared at him as he passed and heatedly said something into the phone that Bash didn't bother hearing.

He stalled at the door, however, the keycard reader flashing red and beeping at him. On the fifth try, the man turned around and said, "Do you mind? I'm having a private conversation with my girlfriend."

Bash took a deep breath, running the card one more time and knowing that if it didn't work, the man would end up with a black eye and a bright plastic phone shoved down his throat. It flashed green and the lock clicked open. He released his held breath and shot the guy a look that made him take a step back before Bash disappeared into his room. He tossed the key on the nightstand and fell onto the bed before the flickering television drew his attention. He closed his eyes for a long time, then sighed. *How the hell do I turn that thing off...?*

Angel could smell the sun coming. After long enough on the street, you learned about stuff like that. The sun was coming soon, and for that Angel was glad.

There had been a shift in the air lately. People were scared of something. They were grouping together, rats fleeing a ship. Angel felt it too, but he didn't believe in safety in numbers. The numbers hadn't helped him when he was overseas, it had made him and everyone around him a target. He was better off on his own. Tucked up underneath the Wilson Street bridge, the roar of the river lulling him in and out of a restless sleep.

He had a good set up. He had been able to procure some sheets, which now hung from the underside of the bridge, creating a sort of tent. He had some food from the local food pantry. A can of peaches was left open from dinner, the sweet scent cutting past the fishy smell of the water, and he gave into temptation deciding breakfast could come early today.

No cars had passed overhead for some time, the bars having closed long ago. But it was nearly time for the first shifters to take over for the third shifters at the local plant, so he wasn't surprised to hear the rumble of cement and rebar adjusting to the weight of a vehicle. It passed over the bridge, the sound of the engine quickly overtaken by the rushing waters. The river was high this time of year, and moved fast and loud out to the lake.

If it had been summer, with a lower water level and less noise, he might have heard them coming. Unfortunately, he did not realize he had company until his eyes landed on a set of feet visible in the small gap between his sheet wall and the ground. Sneakers and dark jeans, standing still just outside of his makeshift tent. He cast a glance around, feeling his heart grow cold as he saw two more sets of shoes, effectively surrounding him. The sheet to his left moved, and then everything went black, the smell of the coming sun replaced with copper and fear.

*Oh shit, I didn't mean for that to work.*

A voice broke through Bash's sleep. He groaned, waking slowly and putting a hand to his throbbing head. The clock on the nightstand read 5:17 AM.

"Damnit," he muttered.

*I mean, the pills - I didn't really want to, you know?* The voice in his head continued, ringing bells of dull pain with each syllable. It clicked into place that the voice belonged to the man with the brightly colored plastic phone.

"What did you think would happen?" Bash spoke aloud into the dark, empty hotel room.

*I just- I thought it might make me feel better to-*

"Do you feel better, moron?" Bash grouched. "Great job."

*I thought it might get her attention...*

"I'm sure she'll bring appetizers to your wake."

*Wake...? But, can't you help me?* the voice plead, louder in his head and full of anguish.

"Guy, if I can hear you, you're well past help," Bash

said. He rolled over in bed and clutched a pillow to his ears, a futile gesture. "Now move along so I can get some sleep."

*Move along…?* The voice was a whisper, as though afraid to be heard now. *Move along where?*

"I got no idea, pal, but the sooner you go, the sooner you're not bothering me."

The voice kept talking, but it was harder for Bash to understand, and it faded away completely just before Bash drifted back to sleep.

# CHAPTER EIGHT

"Jules. Jules. Jules. Jules."

The bed was shaking rhythmically.

"Jules. Jules. Julia." The shaking continued. "Julia. Julia. Jules. Julia."

Julia grabbed the pillow under her head and threw it as hard as she could in the direction of the voice. The shaking stopped and all was indignant silence for a moment before, "Well I'm glad I didn't bring you coffee."

Julia cracked an eye open to see Devin sitting on the end of the bed, shirt and pants dotted with powdered sugar. He pointed toward his feet. "The donut I so generously brought you is on the floor," he glared at her, "next to your gratitude."

"I'm so sorry," she said, slipping out of bed and heading to the bathroom for something to help him clean off. "I'm not a morning person."

"Neither am I, but Detective Dishy stopped by a half hour ago." He dabbed at the powdered spots with the washcloth Julia handed him. "He said that your apartment is ready for you to move back in and that your cat is still an asshole." He looked up at Julia. "He's not wrong, by the way. And he said he would stop by this afternoon, to check in on you." He raised an eyebrow. "I think he likes you."

"It's his job." Julia started gathering her things, she hadn't really unpacked, so there wasn't much to do. "And really? 'He likes you.' Are we in grade school?"

"Fair enough," Devin rolled onto the bed, lying on his stomach. "I think he wants to-"

Another well-aimed pillow cut him off before he could finish his sentence.

Bash was drinking coffee and reading the paper the next morning. It was, he decided, his new ritual. The paper seemed to be stretching the warehouse fire to the limit. The cover was an underdeveloped photo of the warehouse interior, which really didn't show much beyond a pile of ash. He flipped a few pages and landed on the "Upcoming Events" section. Churches battled for the biggest Easter service in about a week and a half. A spring festival downtown. And a celebration at the VFW hall a week or so after that celebrating the fifty-five year anniversary of the German surrender during World War II.

Bash stared at that for a while, the ink blurring and melting into the paper before a shout from the neighboring room broke his concentration. *Oh yeah.* He set the paper on the table and peeked out the door. A woman in a uniform, speaking quickly in a language he didn't know, was backing out of the room to his right, crossing herself. She didn't glance his way, but rather she turned tail and ran off toward the elevator. She had left her cart halfway in the door. Bash slipped his boot off, wedging it in his own door, then squeezed past the cart and into the dead man's room.

He was in his bed, flat on his back with eyes wide open. An empty bottle of prescription pills sat on the nightstand next to a wallet and a single key with a tag that said, "Rental" on it. He flipped the wallet open finding an out-of-state license, a few credit cards, and about one hundred dollars. He flipped to the photos and found only one. A picture of a pretty woman who had been standing with her arm around someone, but that someone had been torn out, and a picture of the dead man was taped to it with inelegant precision.

*Maybe she won't bring appetizers to your wake after all…*

He took the money and the key, and slid past the cart and back into his room before the elevator dinged. Moments later there was commotion aplenty in the hall, and he quietly and quickly began packing his things.

"You're sure you're okay?" Devin was hovering in her kitchen, trying pointedly not to look down at the floor at his feet. It was spotless, but it was hard for her not to flash back to that moment Tabitha had fallen to the ground, blood gushing from her throat. "I can stay if you want me to. The Photo Shack will still be there tomorrow."

Julia set her shoulders. "Yes, I'm sure," she said, her voice sounding far more confident than she expected. "I've got to be okay with it sometime, so it's best to start now."

Devin moved in to hug her, unknowingly planting a foot on the exact spot where her roommate had died. She shook the image away and melted into her friend's embrace. *I will not beg him to stay. I will not beg him to stay.* "Thanks for everything, Devin."

He pulled back, putting his hands on either side of her face and kissing her forehead. "Do not hesitate to call me if you need me. If you're scared, bored, angry, or hungry - call me. I will be here in minutes."

"What if I'm lackadaisical?" she asked.

"You're on your own, don't fucking call me."

She grinned up at him, a warmth in her chest driving away the chill that had been spreading since she walked back into her apartment. "I love you."

"Love you, too, Jules."

A low growl sounded from the hallway.

"And, that's my cue to leave." He hugged her quickly, then slipped out the door.

The cat wandered down the hall and into the kitchen, sniffing the air. "Rufus," Julia chided. "Why are you such an asshole?"


Bash had waited until mid-afternoon to slip out of the hotel. The chaos of the paramedics, police, and hotel insurance lawyers had buzzed outside his room for hours, and he didn't want to risk running into... *what the hell was her name?* Not likely that it mattered anymore. He was leaving that little town and its uncanny coincidences far behind him.

He had been driving for 5 hours when he pulled off the road and into a filling station. The little car he had borrowed had taken some time to get used to. He had traveled on back roads, meandering slowly southward down the coast as he tested brakes, steering, and the automatic transmission. It definitely was not the same as he remembered. Once comfortable enough, he found a busier highway and began following the road signs toward Chicago. The sky had darkened, and the bright glow of the city helped to guide him. Suburban neighborhoods stacked upon each other, turning into urban sprawl and urban decay. The fuel station was brightly lit, and the man behind the counter looked at him from behind plexiglass and steel bars.

"Hey pal," Bash said. "Can I get a pack of Luckies, a city map, and a phone book please?" He slipped a twenty into the little bowl under the bars. "I'll give the phone book back in a sec." The man didn't say anything, taking the money and handing back change, a map, and his smokes.

"No phone book. Check the phone booth outside."

Bash nodded thanks and walked out the door, then down alongside the building to a phone booth. The receiver had been torn out, leaving only a dangling cord, but an immense phone book lay on the ground beneath it. He grabbed it and flipped to the R's. According to the book, Samuel Right lived on Talcott Ave. Checking the map, he found it on the north side of town. He traced the easiest route through the city, committed it to memory, and got back in the car.

*Alright, Sammy, let's hope you have some hospitality for an old friend.*

Angel had been fighting for consciousness for hours, seeing the sun move across the sky in blurred, intermittent time-lapse above him. There was a woman with him, hanging by bound wrists from a tree a few feet away, blood pooling below her dangling feet. She had whimpered when the taller of the coal-eyed monsters made the first shallow cuts, but had been silent ever since.

They were at the top of a dune. In his rare moments of lucidity he could hear the waves far below them and feel the wind coming off the lake. His blood, dripping slowly from several cuts on his arms, had coated his sides, sticky on his clothes, and cold. He was so cold.

It was dark now, but he could see the woman across from him in the light of the torches. She was pale, and the pool of blood at her feet was far larger than it should be for such a small body. There were eight kids now, standing in a circle and staring at the both of them with empty eyes. He heard someone talking, but the sound came from far away and under water. His vision was blurring again. A dark shadow appeared in front of the woman, shaking her roughly. The body, as she was definitely now just a body, swayed with the motion.

"Goddamnit!" the curse was mostly clear, laced with anger and frustration, and floated through the water to him. The shadow turned to him, gesturing and shouted something that was lost to the waves. One of the black-eyed teens lifted a blade and came toward him.

Angel breathed as deep as he could through his nose, smelling the faintest trace of the sunrise, before the heat of the blade across his throat warmed his ice cold body, and everything faded away for good.

## PART TWO
## INTERLUDE – SPRING 1994

Rachel sat at the kitchen table, using her small fingers to spread acrylic paint across an oversized piece of paper, and maybe a little on the table. In the living room, her sister sat on the couch with Rob, The Boyfriend, giggling with canned laughter on the television. It was Friday night, and her sister was over to watch her while her parents went out to some kind of party. Elizabeth was nineteen and lived in a dorm an hour away, but she often visited, which made Rachel happy.

Rob's inclusion did *not* make Rachel happy. He didn't seem to have time or patience for the six-nearly-seven-year-old little sister, and Elizabeth didn't seem to notice. Rachel spread a little more of the purple on the top of the wooden table, watching the paint seep into the grain. *Oops.* She smiled.

Fake audience laughter mixed with Rob's loud chuckle and soft footfalls as Elizabeth wandered into the room. "Almost bedtime, kiddo," she said, opening the fridge.

Rachel frowned. "But you said we could play Sorry tonight."

Her sister frowned back. "It's a little too late now, Rach. Maybe tomorrow?"

Rachel felt tears well in her eyes and rubbed the back of her hand against them. "You always say that."

Elizabeth knelt down to her level and pushed hair out of her little sister's face. "And I always mean it. Sometimes I just get busy. I'm in college now, and things get a little crazy. You'll under-"

A knock at the door interrupted her sentence. She sighed. "Rob, can you get that? It's probably the pizza."

Rachel's frown grew. "You ordered pizza? I ate microwave Spaghettios!"

Elizabeth frowned back, hearing Rob's movement toward the front door. "Alright, Rachel it's time for bed."

Rachel stood opening her mouth to argue when Rob's shout sliced through the air.

"What the fu-" his words were cut off in a strangled gurgling that sent a jolt of pure primal fear through Rachel's chest. She looked at her sister and saw the color drain from her face.

"Elizabeth?" Rachel's voice was small, as though she were four-nearly-five, not six-nearly-seven. "What's going on?"

Her sister stepped cautiously to the left, peeking through the archway between the kitchen and living room, where her line of sight would let her see the front door beyond. Rachel watched the confusion turn to horror on Elizabeth's face before she found herself swept into her sister's arms. Rachel looked over Elizabeth's shoulder as the older girl ran through the expansive kitchen and to the back door. Two shadows were in the living room, walking toward them at a slow, deliberate pace. The light from the television flashed off a long knife one of them was carrying, and Rachel could see that it was stained with a dripping red.

Elizabeth made it to the back door, threw it open and screamed. Rachel turned her head to see what her sister saw. Two more hooded figures stood in the doorway. They turned their heads up so the bright kitchen light hit their faces. Blank faces and black eyes watched them as Elizabeth stumbled backward.

"Let us in," they said together and stepped across the threshold.

# CHAPTER NINE

Sue Ellen Right put the last dish in the dish drainer and pulled the string above the sink to kill the light. She wiped her hands on a dish towel, then looped it back through the handle on the oven, sure to lay it flat so it dried properly. She had just clicked on the television and snuggled into the couch to settle in for her nightly shows when the doorbell rang. She assumed that it was the night nurse, and yelled, "C'mon in, Terry!" When nothing happened, she groaned and pulled herself off the couch.

The person at the door was not the night nurse. He was a young man, maybe in his mid-twenties, with sandy hair in need of a cut. He was tall, but not imposing, and he gave her a beauteous smile. "Good evening, ma'am," he said. "I'm looking for a Mr. Samuel Right."

She squinted at him, trying to place his face. He looked familiar. "That's my father," she said. "Who are you?"

The man offered his hand to her. "My name is Bash," he said. "Your father fought in WWII, correct? 8th

Infantry Division?"

It clicked then where she recognized him. An old photo of her dad with his squad in Ireland before they shipped over to France. Nine men in total, including her father and a man that looked strikingly like the young man on her doorstep. "Yes," she said, and stepped aside, letting him in. "Oh yes, he was. Are you like a- a grandson of one of his old war buddies or something?"

"Something like that," Bash said. "Is there any way I can see him?"

She nodded, frowning. "You can, but I'm not certain you're going to get much in the way of conversation." She led him down a hall. "He had a stroke a year ago, poor thing. He's been bedridden ever since, and he doesn't really talk much anymore."

"I understand," Bash said.

Sue Ellen opened a door spilling dim lamp light into the darkened hall. "Dad?" she said softly. "Are you awake? There's someone here to see you."

Her father was propped up on pillows. He looked withered, wisps of white hair sticking out around his head. His eyes were fixed on a flickering television at the end of the bed, though the volume was almost completely down. He turned his head as they walked in, focusing first on Sue Ellen, then Bash. He blinked, then blinked again.

"Sarge?" he said, voice breaking for lack of use. "Sarge?"

"No, Dad," Sue Ellen said. "This is Bash, he's your friend's grandson."

Her father stared at the stranger with eyes wide. His mouth moved but no further words escaped. Bash went to his bedside, putting a hand on the old man's arm.

"You see?" Sue Ellen said softly, then sighed. "Wait here, I'll go get that photograph." She left the room for a few moments, and when she came back, her father was clutching the young man's hand. Bash was crouched next to him, whispering to him. "Is everything okay?" she asked.

"Of course," the young man said, straightening up.

Sue Ellen looked down at the photo, and then back at the man. "The resemblance between you and your grandfather is astounding," she said and handed him the frame.

Bash took it, jaw set as he studied it for a moment before speaking. "You know, only six of these men made it as far as Hurtgen Forest," he said softly.

Sue Ellen shook her head, "Dad never talked about it much."

Her father reached for the frame, pulling it out of Bash's hands. Sue Ellen noticed that there were tears near spilling from the corners of his eyes as he struggled with the back of the frame, trying to pry it off. Bash leaned in to help, and soon the frame was open and a piece of paper fell onto the blanket. The old man picked it up, unfolded it, and pushed it toward Bash's hand. The younger man picked it up, looking at it.

"What is that?" Sue Ellen asked.

"Names and addresses," Bash said. "Three of them." The names were written in faded black ink, some even had more than one address. When a new address was added, the old one had been scratched out.

Sue Ellen peeked at it. "Oh yes," she said. "Dad visited the remaining squad once a year every year from the time they shipped home until," she paused, "well until this year."

Her father pointed at Bash, then at the paper, his face stern.

"Okay," Bash whispered. He took Samuel's hand in his. "Okay, I got it." He folded the paper and tucked it away in his back pocket. He squeezed the man's hand one more time, before turning to leave.

"Well," Sue Ellen said, leading him back to the front door. "Thanks for coming to visit him. I think it means a lot to him."

The young man cleared his throat, stepping outside before turning back to her and offering her a smile that didn't quite touch his eyes. "Means a lot to me, too, ma'am. Thank you." He nodded at her and turned on his heel, heading back out into the darkened city street.

Julia was in her own home, on her own couch, in her comfy pajamas, watching her favorite films on her own VCR, and she was terrified.

Every light in the house was on, and she couldn't decide if the door to the spare room was scarier open, or closed. The curtains on every window were pulled shut, the windows locked tight. She debated nailing them all shut, but convinced herself that she might want her security deposit back someday, so she didn't.

Fifteen minutes later her movie was finished, and she had a hammer in one hand and a box of nails in the other when there was a knock at the door. She jumped, dropping the nails to the floor, nearly stabbing her pinky toe in the process.

"Julia?" came the voice. "Are you okay?"

She clutched the hammer and tiptoed around the spilled nails to peek out the peephole in the door. "Cole?"

"Yeah." There was a beat. "But I also now answer to Detective Dishy."

Julia felt her face flush, but she threw open the door anyway. "Hi," she said brightly. "Come on in!"

His smile looked tired as he walked into her apartment. He looked down at his feet unconsciously as he made his way over the spot where the body had been a few days earlier, and stood in the kitchen away from her accidental nail piles. "Where's your cat?" he asked. The realization that he'd spent more time in her apartment the last few days than she had was disconcerting.

"He's sleeping in my room," Julia said. "You should be safe for now."

Cole laughed and put his hands in his pockets. "Sorry about the late visit," he said. "I won't take up much of your time, I just wanted to stop in and check on you." He studied her face for a moment. "How are you?"

She took a breath, held it briefly, then blurted out, "I'm scared to death, actually."

Cole's face fell. "I'm so sorry, Julia." He put a hand on her shoulder. "There are two officers with your parking lot on their rotation tonight. Is there anything else I can do to help you feel better?" He put his hands back in his pockets.

*You are a strong, independent young woman,* Julia thought to herself. *You do not need anything from him.* "No," she said softly. "No, I'm okay."

"Okay." He took a business card from his pocket and set it on her kitchen counter. "Here's my number, again, if you need me for anything at all."

She nodded her good-byes and watched him go out the door. She still had the hammer in her hand, and she set it down gently next to his business card. Her hand twitched above them both, deliberating which to pick up.

Cole was almost to his car when his phone rang. "This is Detective Cole," he said.

"I need you to come back," Julia said. "I've got an article to write, and your knowledge of how the police are handling this case is integral." She paused. "There will be snacks."

Cole smiled, turning around and looking back at Julia's building. "Well, I can't say no to snacks."

***

# From the Message Boards

## Topic: Boston BEK Story

**ThermoDina** *1-29-2000, 12:39am*
I remember seeing that Owen kid on the milk cartons. Y'all are freaking me out. That can't be real.

**Forgotten1968** *1-29-2000, 9:08am*
It's very real. Owen went to a better place.

**ThermoDina** *1-29-2000, 9:30am*
You mean, like Heaven?

**Forgotten1968** *1-29-2000, 10:16am*
No, a real place. Far better than any heaven you could dream of.

**Raccoon** *1-29-2000, 11:46am*
Dude, you need meds...

***

# CHAPTER TEN

Bash was in the middle of Chicago with a grumbling stomach, a half tank of fuel, and very little cash. The town had changed a bit since last he was there, but the vibrancy of the evening still hummed through the streets just as he remembered.

He found a restaurant that looked promising on the first floor of a chain hotel and a parking spot three blocks away. He rifled through his bags and grabbed a navy blue button-up dress shirt that didn't appear to be too wrinkled. He swapped it for the plain t-shirt he'd been wearing for his trip and looked at himself in the reflective glass of the car window. It would have to do. There was a slight chill in the air, but he put his hands in the pockets of his dark jeans and began walking.

The restaurant was casual but definitely catered to the upper middle class. He nodded at the greeter, "I was just hoping to grab a bite and a drink, is there a seat free at the bar?"

The greeter fluttered her hands in the direction of the bar with the utmost disinterest. "Have at it."

Bash nodded and moved past her. The bar area was dimly lit and busy with a row of tables along one side, and bar stools squeezed in atop one another at the bar side. He scanned the room, then planted himself in an empty stool adjacent to a table of six women who were on the far side of sobriety and the early stages of bad decision-making. He ordered a pint of stout and a burger and settled in, listening passively to their conversation.

It was "Girls' Night" evidently, as they toasted to "Girls' Night" once every few minutes with raucous laughter. One of them, a blonde caught his eye after one of their toasts and he offered a smile and lifted his glass. By the time he was done with his burger, the girls had struck up a conversation with him. He learned their names (which he promptly forgot) and their drinks (which had vulgar names) and he was asked to sit with them for a few toasts. The asinine drinks that they plied him with were sweet and potent, and he started slipping them onto the empty table next to them rather than drink them after the first two rounds.

"You guys," the brunette sitting across from him put a hand over her mouth, whispering loudly, "that guy over there is creeping me out."

Bash glanced in the direction she gestured and saw a man sitting alone at a high top toward the end of the bar. He was middle-aged, had a briefcase and a suit and a thin mustache in compensation for the lack of hair atop his head. He was definitely staring at the table of young women, and he didn't look away until he noticed Bash looking back. A familiar thrill fluttered to life in his mind, followed by an equally familiar cool-water calm that started in his spine and moved outward, settling in his smile.

"Excuse me, ladies." He stood from the table, and walked with purpose to the staring man's table, sitting down across from him and blocking his view. Bash noted the tell-tale bleariness in his eyes and estimated him to be a few hours past his first drink of the night.

"You stare any harder and I'm going to have to charge you."

The man sputtered. "Ch- charge?" He wiped a napkin across his forehead. "I don't know what you're talking about."

Bash lit a cigarette. "Yeah, you do." He glanced back at the girls, most of them had turned their attention back to each other, but one of the girls, a leggy redhead, arched a brow at him. He turned back to the man. "These girls don't come cheap."

The man deliberated, eyes wandering back to the women with a hollow lecherousness that soured Bash's stomach. "I want the redhead."

Bash nodded, "$700 for an hour, $3500 for the whole night."

"Just an hour," the man said, eyes fixed on the group of girls. "And the blonde. Both of them."

"That's $2000 for the hour, then," Bash said. The man looked at him, disappointed. "This is not a two-for-one kinda business, pal. It's $2000 for two girls for one hour."

"Ok." He pulled his billfold from his briefcase and discreetly counted out twenty hundred dollar bills. He passed it to Bash but didn't let go. "Anything goes, right?"

Bash suppressed a shudder, but smiled at the man. "Sure, pal. Whatever you want." The man released the bills and Bash slipped them into his front pocket. "Pay your tab here, then head up to your room. I'll bring the girls up in twenty minutes. What room number?"

The man was openly leering again. "1214."

Bash nodded, then turned and sauntered back to the

table of women. "He's paying his tab and leaving. Shouldn't be a bother again."

They erupted in a round of cheers and laughter. The leggy redhead stood, gesturing to the seat next to her, and putting a hand on his arm. "Have a seat, hero. I'm going to get you a drink you're actually going to like." She cast a sidelong glance at the four  discarded shots he'd dropped at the nearby table. "Scotch, neat?"

He felt a genuine smile pull at the corners of his mouth. "On the rocks," he said. "Gotta keep my wits about me around you ladies."

Her eyes narrowed and her red lips turned up in a smirk, "I bet you do."

Charlotte the bartender wasn't surprised to see the drunken businessman stumble back into the bar an hour after he'd left, red-faced and boiling around the collar. Most remorseful drunks would try leaving early in the night, only to come back later and hit the booze twice as hard. It surprised her, however, that the drunk went directly toward the table of women at the end of the bar and started yelling.

"What the hell are they still doing here?" he asked, gesturing to a redhead and a blonde that sat on either side of the attractive young man who had come in solo (and by the looks of it, likely wouldn't leave that way) earlier in the night. The drunk reached out a hand to the blond. "I was supposed to be the filling in a slut sandwich by now!"

Charlotte reached for the phone, dialing hotel security, speaking the code in quickly before hanging up. The young man at the girls' table knocked the man's hand away from the blonde, and stood slowly, facing the drunk. "I believe I told you to go to your room and stay there," he said, voice low and calm. "Your behavior is inappropriate in front of these women."

The drunken man sputtered. "But- but they're whores!"

The punch came as soon as the words were out of his mouth. One minute the man was spewing out profanities, and the next he was half-conscious on the floor. The sandy-haired man looked up at Charlotte. "I trust you have people that can handle this from here?"

"Already on their way," she said.

The young man nodded, turning back to the table. "You ladies alright? I apologize, I really thought he would listen to my sound advice."

The blonde looked shocked, her lips were quivering as she asked, "What advice?"

The man looked grave, "That if he didn't leave you girls alone, I would cold-cock him."

Charlotte turned her attention away from the now giggling again group of girls and focused on the security guards that were entering the bar. "Is it the guy on the floor?" one of them asked.

Charlotte frowned. "Yes," she said. "Get him to his room and make sure he stays there."

The guards nodded and picked the man up. He groaned something about whores and money, but no one paid him much mind. *It's always something,* she thought and began pouring a complimentary round of drinks for the girls' table.


"Look, I may have been exaggerating when I said snacks," Julia said. The plate she set on the coffee table had three stacks of club crackers, near toppling, and a very small handful of red grapes. "I also have a half carton of definitely expired milk, if that's your thing."

Cole laughed and leaned forward, grabbing a grape and popping it in his mouth. "Totally understandable."

He was without his jacket for the first time since Julia had met him. Underneath he had a pale blue button-up with the top buttons undone and a loosened tie. Disheveled, Julia decided, was a perpetual state with Detective Cole. However, she was still in her pajamas, so she had no room to talk.

She set two bottles of beer on the table, then sat on the other side of the couch, turning sideways to face him. "So, Detective," she said, twisting off the cap of her bottle. "What have you found so far in The Case of the Singed Photojournalist?"

Cole barked out a laugh, head thrown back. "Totally off the record, right?"

"Of course!" she grinned, pulling her legs underneath her.

Cole took a drink. "Well actually," he said. "I found the knife you used to cut yourself free, and another officer found the Knox kid's wallet. We got three sets of prints off the knife and two sets of prints off the wallet, so I sent those out to compare to the database. I'm hoping we'll get a few hits."

"Really?" Julia raised her eyebrows. "When will you have results?"

"Anytime really," he said. "I'll get an email when they come in. I could check it if you don't mind me using your computer."

"Sure, no problem." Julia hopped up and went to her computer, tapping the space bar and waiting for it to wake up. "I've got dial-up, so it'll be a minute."

Cole nodded and took a drink, wincing as the screech of the modem filled the air. "I went down the rabbit hole last night looking up black-eyed kid sightings and theories."

Julia chuckled softly, "It's easy to do." She was silent for a moment, waiting for the noise to die off. As it did, her website began to load, little dancing ghosts popping up on the screen.

Cole came up behind her. "That's a good site. I spent a lot of time on that one last night."

"Thank you," she said. "It's mine. That reminds me I have to make a post about what happened at the warehouse." Her thoughts strayed to that night, pondering how best to write it up. "Oh! I saw that guy again, the transient. Devin and I bought him a drink at the hotel last night."

"Oh yeah?" Cole frowned. "Did you find anything out about him?"

"Not really." She stood, turning the chair to face him. "He did say something about being in the war."

"So he's in his thirties?"

"He looks my age probably. But he said looks were deceiving," Julia said, feeling an exasperation creep into her lungs. "He didn't seem apt to give much information."

"Let me know if he shows up again," he said. He sat at the desk and typed in an address. The page was simple, and it loaded without much wait time. Julia averted her eyes while he typed in his login and waited for his email to populate. "Got it!" he said a few minutes later.

Julia leaned down near him, looking at the screen. "The wallet had Knox's prints and another set. The knife had a set that matched the second on the wallet and two other sets. One set had to be yours, and they didn't register in the database." Cole said, looking up at her. "That just means you've never been fingerprinted for any reason, be it being arrested or being in the military, what have you."

Julia nodded. "So did the other prints on the knife show up as anything?"

Cole shook his head. "This doesn't make a whole hell

of a lot of sense," he muttered. "The only set that hit was the set that was on both the knife and the wallet. And those belong to," he paused, squinting at the screen, "Boyd Mingus. We've got his prints from the Army database…"

"Okay," Julia said. "What's weird about that?"

"He joined in 1942, and was killed in action in Germany in 1944," Cole said. He put his hand over his mouth, pulling down as if to pull whatever secret was missing out of the top of his head.

Julia straightened. "Yeah. That's weird." She turned and headed toward the kitchen, pulling the last four beers from the fridge and bringing them back to the desk. "Help yourself."

Cole did, popping the cap open and leaning back. "I mean, even if he wasn't killed, that would still make him at least seventy years old."

Julia took a drink, "So we're looking for the poster boy for the AARP who is also the ringleader of a group of supernatural black-eyed kids." She shrugged. "Could be weirder."

Cole looked at her incredulously.

She shrugged again. "Could be zombies or dragons or something, I don't know. Trying to look at the bright side." She laughed with a hint of hysteria and took another drink.

# CHAPTER ELEVEN

Bash stirred, dreams and nightmares chasing him out of sleep and into unfamiliar surroundings. A bright white cloud of feather-filled comforter was piled atop his chest. Beyond that were light blue interior walls and the typical generic layout of a hotel room. He moved the comforter away, the heat of it too much for him, and found an extra arm he wasn't expecting draped across his stomach. His movement triggered the arm to pull back, dragging tapered red nails lightly along his bare skin. His gaze followed the arm up past the elbow, to the pale, freckled shoulder and a pleasant mass of red hair. *Oh yeah,* Bash thought to himself, *I know where I am now.* He smiled and shifted, pulling himself away from the redhead, swinging his legs off the bed and sitting up to light a cigarette.

The redhead sighed, and he felt her weight shifting on the bed as she sat up as well. "Mind if I have one of those?"

He turned, handing her one and lighting it for her. "G'morning," he said.

She had the pure white comforter pulled up around

her, hair spilling down in a mess of contrasting color. "Good morning," she said, taking a drag from the cigarette and coughing. "Ugh, why did I ask for this?" She handed it back to him, and he snuffed it out in the ashtray on the side table.

"Not a smoker?" he asked.

She pulled herself out of bed, the comforter still wrapped tightly around her. "Not anymore," she said. "Those things will kill you."

Bash looked at the cigarette in his hand, pondering. "Huh," he said. "No shit?" He shrugged, taking another drag. "Somethin's bound to kill me eventually, I guess."

The redhead started coffee brewing in the small pot next to the television while Bash finished his cigarette. "Where are you heading to, hero?" she asked.

He looked back at the bed, and then at the half-naked woman, and he wondered if he really had to head anywhere just yet. He stood, grabbing his jeans and reaching into the pocket, he pulled out the piece of paper that Samuel Right had given him the evening before. Opening it, he calculated the closest address on the list. "Looks like I'm heading to Minnesota," he said.

She didn't ask why, or when, but instead brought him a cup of black coffee and sat next to him on the bed, cradling her own mug between her palms. She smelled like cinnamon. Bash looked down at his list, then at one long, pale leg that peeked out from under the comforter, then back at the list. He sighed and reached for his jeans again, about to pull them on and make his exit.

"So," she said. "Out of curiosity, how much money did you end up getting off that guy?"

Bash froze, one leg in and one leg out of his pants. "What guy?"

He met her gaze and watched her eyebrow arch and her mouth purse prettily with a look that screamed, "Oh come on, now."

He let go of the jeans, turning fully toward her, and smiling. "I got enough," he said, "for now." He leaned in, putting his hands on the bed on either side of her legs. "Why?"

She smirked at him, reaching to set her coffee mug on the side table. "Just curious how lucrative such heroic deeds were these days." Her tone was playful, mocking, and far more tempting than Bash had the willpower to deny.

He closed the short distance between them and kissed her, letting the folded up paper of addresses fall to the floor to be pursued later.

The basement of the Grand River Tribune building had always unnerved Julia. A series of dimly lit hallways that were thick with a malaise of stagnant time. The walls were bare, giving her nothing to mark the distance she'd walked. Her destination, the end of the hall, felt still miles away.

There was an adjacent hallway 20 feet ahead on her right. Deep shadows spilled out onto the cracked, ancient tile floor. A dark electricity filled the air as she neared it, standing the hair at the back of her neck on end. She wanted to squeeze her eyes shut and run, but she was a grown woman who would not succumb to her overactive imagination. She trudged on, eyes forward toward her goal.

Two of them, a tall boy and a younger girl with straw-colored braids, were waiting for her in that hallway. She saw their movement out of the corner of her eye and turned just in time to block the slashing knife aimed at her ribcage. Pain laced through her hand as the blade tore across her knuckles, and a scream erupted from her throat at the pain and fear.

She pushed the younger one away, moving to run, but the taller one, the boy, grabbed her around the wrist, spinning her around to face him. Black eyes and an inhuman grin.

"Julia, please!"

Julia kicked out, aiming for his knee and making contact.

Her attacker yelped. "Julia, please wake up. You're hurting yourself. And me!"

Julia stilled, the scene in front of her losing focus. Her consciousness rushed forward until her eyes popped open. She was sitting up in her bed. Cole was perched awkwardly in front of her, hands wrapped around her wrists. "Cole?"

"Julia?" he whispered. He let go of one of her arms and brought a hand up to her face, brushing damp hair out of her eyes. "Are you in there?"

She took a deep breath, gasping in cool air as though she'd been trapped in a furnace instead of a dream. She felt heavy sobs in her chest, stretching her throat before they escaped with a flood of tears.

Cole moved swiftly, adjusting to sit next to her, and wrapped an arm around her shoulders. She curled herself into a ball and allowed the sobs to take over in the hopes that they would wash away her night terrors. Tentatively he put his other arm around her, holding her until the shudders subsided.

Several minutes later, Julia sniffled pulling away from him and casting her glance down. She wiped at her eyes. "I'm sorry," she said.

He shifted away giving her space. "Jesus, Julia, don't be sorry. You've been through a lot the last few days. No one would expect you to be unaffected by that."

Julia nodded and sniffed. Taking in her surroundings. Rain and curtains stifled the morning light to a dim haze.

Cole was wearing his jacket, the smell of the soft leather was comforting. The night before came back to her then, his offer to stay on the couch until morning, keeping watch. He had known she was scared to be alone. That was hard enough to admit, but this morning, letting him comfort her as though she were a child while she cried about bad dreams. Shame rushed through her and she swallowed hard.

Cole frowned and stood, taking her hand. "Come on," he said with a smile. "I'm going to make you breakfast."

Twenty minutes later Cole sat a plate of scrambled eggs and toast in front of Julia. He refilled her coffee mug, then sat down across from her with his own plate. "So, have you had night terrors before?" he asked before shoveling eggs onto his toast and taking a large bite.

Julia nodded, sipping her coffee. She looked so tired, vulnerable and afraid, as though she still felt the monsters lapping at her heels. "I had them for years after my dad was killed and Gene disappeared." She picked at her eggs and took a bite. "These are really good," she said, surprise in her voice. She evidently hadn't meant to sound so surprised, as her cheeks flushed red and her eyes widened.

Cole laughed. "Thanks a lot," he said.

Julia sighed, looking down at her plate. "I'm going back to bed so I can start this day over again, hopefully without all the embarrassment."

"You're fine," Cole scoffed. "My scrambled eggs are shockingly delicious - it's understandable." He finished his eggs, not asking any further questions. He studied her without staring, watching to make sure she was really all right.

He had been in the process of writing her a quick

note and leaving when her screams had started. He'd rushed into her room to find her alone, but fighting against a devil he couldn't see. She thrashed, punching out, and had bloodied a knuckle against her bedside table already before he'd gotten there.

Julia finished her eggs and took her plate and his to the kitchen sink, rinsing them before putting them in the dishwasher. He followed her, doing the same with the pan and spatula he had used. She pushed the button on the washer and sighed, leaning against the counter. Cole noticed the dried blood on her hand. He got a paper towel, wet it with warm water and took her hand in his to clean it off. "Thank you, Cole," she said. "Again. For everything."

She was looking brighter now, like she had looked when he first saw her at the Knox house crime scene. *God, that was less than a week ago*, he thought absently. Her eyes were clearer, the darkness of her dreams fading. A few strands of silver-blond hair had fallen across her cheek, and he reached forward to tuck them back behind her ear without thinking.

He opened his mouth, then closed it, forgetting what he had meant to say. His fingers lingered on her face as she looked up at him. "Julia, I-" A knock at the door interrupted him. Cole stepped back, not realizing he had stepped forward. "I'm sorry, but I should go," he said quickly. "My poor dog has probably torn my house apart by now."

Julia took a breath, then smiled. "You have a dog?" she asked.

"He's more like a lazy end table with a shedding problem," Cole said. "But yes."

The knock sounded again, startling both of them this time. Cole looked at Julia and she nodded. He opened the door to see Devin, who looked him up and down, looked pointedly at his watch, and then raised his eyebrows. "You're here early, Detective."

Cole fought to contain the stammering that threatened to bubble out of his mouth, instead saying, "As are you." He turned to Julia who looked like she was stifling a laugh. "Miss Winters, feel free to call any time."

Julia nodded. "Thank you, Detective."

He rolled his eyes, looking at her. "Have a good morning, Julia," he said, catching her smirk as he brushed past Devin and left her apartment.

# CHAPTER TWELVE

"Okay, put the cleaning supplies down. You've been out-damned-spot-ing for the last hour. I promise you, there's nothing there anymore, Lady Macbeth."

Julia looked at the cabinets and the floor where the blood had splattered. Of course, there was nothing there. Cole had made sure the best cleaners had come in after the crime scene tape came down. But that didn't stop her from seeing it in her mind's eye every time she looked at the spot where Tabitha had died.

"Yeah. You're right," she said and tossed the towel into the sink.

"I usually am," Devin said. "Now when is your first appointment?"

Julia had put an ad in the paper for a new roommate the previous morning and had already gotten some calls about it. Devin had come over to help her interview the potentials. "Noon," she said and glanced at the clock. "So she should be here soon."

Devin nodded. "So… the room is empty? I mean, everything's been cleaned out?"

"Yeah. Cole let Tabitha's brother in to get her stuff while I was still at the hotel. There wasn't a lot, I guess."

"And your bastard cat?"

Julia laughed. "He's in my room for the time being." There was a knock on the door. Julia pushed herself away from the counter. "But he is a significant hurdle in this whole roommate business." Rufus the cat had tolerated Cole's presence for the evening, but Julia suspected that may be because Cole had fed the cat for the last couple days. Rufus was practical that way.

She took a breath, putting a hand on the doorknob, and prepared herself for a very long afternoon.

Cole was regretting the eggs he'd had that morning. His stomach churned at the sight before him. He was on a wooded plateau at the top of a dune. The sand at his feet was stained deep brown. Two people, a man and woman, were hanging above him, arms bound and over their heads, feet dangling and blood-covered. Their faces, bent toward the ground at an unnatural angle, were gray and drawn, sunken in and completely without life. "Any idea who they are?"

Biggs pulled a flashlight from the pocket of her jacket. "No one has reported anyone missing. And these guys have been out here all night. Unless someone comes looking for them soon, I'm going assume they're homeless."

Cole nodded grimly. "Let me know if you find anything."

"Sure thing, Cole," she said and moved to the perimeter of the crime scene, turning her flashlight on and pointing it at the ground. The beam swept back and forth slowly, hypnotizing Cole for a moment before he shook himself and turned to leave.

There was no doubt in his mind that this was the

same people that had attacked Julia and the Knox kid. *What the hell are they doing?* It was ritualistic, it would seem, unless the little bastards were just sadists.

A flash caught his eye and he turned to see a young man holding what looked like a brand new digital camera taking pictures at the edge of the crime scene tape. He frowned and walked purposefully toward him. "Nope," he said. "Sorry - no press. You're gonna have to leave."

The guy fumbled with his lanyard. It bore the same credentials that Julia's had. "But I-"

"Nope," Cole said again, standing in front of him and shooing him back the way he had come. "Gotta go. Get."

The kid scowled at him, but turned and walked toward the path.

Biggs appeared behind him, eyebrow raised. "What was that about?" she asked.

"We don't need this in the paper just yet. We need to find out who these people were before their corpses are plastered on the front page," Cole said, turning away to head toward the path leading back down the dune. *Or possibly I'm playing favorites. Hard to tell...*

It was a grave.

Bash looked at the folded up piece of paper in his hand. The address had led him here, to Spring Grove Cemetery, on the outskirts of a very small town in southern Minnesota. He now stood in front of the headstone bearing the name attached to that address.

Richard Waterston
PFC US Army
World War II
Oct 13, 1920 - Jan 3, 1998

The headstone was simple. No mention of a spouse or children, but there was a granite flower pot that looked freshly weeded, and the flag planted in it seemed pristine. Someone was taking care of him, still. Bash crouched and brushed a small pile of grass clippings off the side of the stone. He laid his hand on the cold granite for a moment, staring at the carved words, studying the shadows the afternoon sun cast. "Seventy-seven years," Bash mused. "Not a shabby spread, Dick. I hope it was a good one."

He stood, dusting his hands off on his jeans, and walked back to the car. He would be heading south on I-35 into Kansas, if he remembered correctly, some of the flattest country he had ever seen. He stretched, looking around at the fields surrounding the cemetery, budding bright greens swaying slowly in the breeze. He had a long way to go, and while he wasn't in a hurry, the expiration date on his stolen vehicle was sure to come up sooner than later. He got in the car and started the engine. The news radio he had been listening to blared to life and he turned it off. Information overload on the way to Minnesota had left him feeling dizzy, but none of the music stations played anything he could convince himself to enjoy. The silence got to him before he found the highway, however, and he turned the news back on, lowering the volume to a dull chatter that would keep him company into the evening.

# CHAPTER THIRTEEN

Julia shut the door to her apartment, leaning heavily back on it with a sigh. "Well," she said. "Maybe tomorrow will be better."

"I'm not sure it can get worse," Devin intoned. "Though the girl was sweet."

"Sweet, but not bright," Julia said. "The ad says there are cats in the apartment. Why the hell would you bother calling if you're deathly allergic?"

"If it's a choice between Our Lady of the Infinite Sneeze and Sir Ogglesalot, get rid of the cat." Devin gestured toward the closed door where moments earlier Julia had ushered out a young man who had been more interested in looking at her than at the apartment.

Julia scowled. "I'm not getting rid of the cat. I've got another person coming tomorrow afternoon, he'll work out, I'm sure."

Before Devin could respond, there was a knock at the door. "It's Cole," the voice on the other side called.

She opened the door. "Come on in."

"I can't stay," he said. "I just wanted to let you know

109

that there was another incident."

Julia's stomach dropped. "What?"

Cole shook his head. "I can't tell you much about it, we don't know much yet. But I wanted to make sure you heard about it from me." He glanced at Devin. "And if you can avoid being alone tonight, I think that would put us both at ease."

Julia looked back at her friend, who grinned widely and said, "Sleepover!"

The fear in her gut kept her from returning the enthusiasm, but she was thankful he was staying. "Looks like I'm set."

"Good," he said. "You'll be safe. I'll check in again tomorrow, if that's ok?"

She offered a nervous smile. "Of course."

He turned to go but stuck his head back through the door before it shut. "Oh, there was a photographer from the paper - young kid, nice camera, kinda looked like he's fresh from a gap year in Europe. He a friend of yours?"

"No," Julia said. "Hate him."

"Good. Then I don't feel bad about evicting him from the crime scene." He gave her a wave, then disappeared out the door.

Devin swiveled on his chair and grinned at Julia. "Do we start with board games and beer or video games and vodka?"

The old man was sitting on his porch, a beer in one hand and a cigarette in the other, watching the evening people walk by. His face didn't change when Bash turned off the main sidewalk, up the path and onto the porch steps. The man took a drink, studying him.

"You Death?" he asked, his voice gruff.

Bash chuckled. "Not last I checked."

The old man nodded and gestured to a chair that sat

across from him. "Have a seat."

Bash did as he was told, pulling a cigarette from his pocket. "How've you been, Williams?"

"Old," he said.

Bash laughed and leaned forward to ash in the ashtray on the small round table between them.

Williams reached next to him and grabbed a bottle of beer from a hidden cooler, offering it to Bash. "Still a teetotaller?"

Bash shook his head. "Decidedly, no." He took the bottle and popped the cap off. He could feel the old man's eyes on him as he took the first drink.

"Been to see Sam?" he asked.

Bash nodded. "And Dick."

Williams cleared his throat. "Jefferson's six feet under as well, if you didn't know that already. Took his own life twelve years ago."

Bash shook his head, looking down. "Sorry to hear that."

"He was one of those that never really left the war, you see. Dick, he went back to Minnesota to his wife and daughter, and they ran the family farm. Kept him busy. Samuel, he had all that new money back then, and he invested wisely. Had a nice family. But Jefferson - he didn't have much after he came back. Then he went to Korea, and came back even stranger." He took a drink, wiping his mouth with the back of his hand and taking a drag of the nearly-out cigarette. "We tried to help, but I don't think it ever made much of a difference."

They sat in silence for a while. Listening to the night sounds of the busy main street.

"We saw you," the old man said, startling Bash out of the peaceful silence. "You and Carv. You were pinned down in that barn. We saw the shell hit - no way you survived that."

Bash put out his cigarette and met the man's eyes, saying nothing.

"Yet, here you are." Williams coughed, tossing his finished cigarette and lighting another. "You left us."

Bash felt a very old wound, hidden deep inside, shift and rupture. "That wasn't the plan," he said.

"Not the plan, maybe, but it was the outcome. Four of us left in the middle of a battle without a commanding officer. Mourning you and Carv. But here you are."

Bash felt like there should be anger behind the words, but he didn't hear it in the man's voice. That didn't make the words any easier to swallow.

"What about you?" Bash said.

"What about me?" gruffed the old man.

"Dick ran a farm. Sam invested wisely. Jefferson went off the deep end. What about you?"

For the first time, the old man's face broke into a smile. A warm, fond smile that showed every year etched across his face. "I was a history teacher. My wife was the music teacher. We lived here," he motioned behind him at the old Victorian home, "for fifty years before she passed a couple summers ago. We've got seven kids and twenty-two grandbabies." The smile didn't fade as he met Bash's gaze. "I've had a very, very good life."

Another, very different wound deep within him twitched, pulling at a scar poorly healed. But he met the man's smile with one of his own. "That's good to hear."

"What about you?" Williams asked.

Bash straightened, pondering. "That's a long story."

The old man stood, motioning Bash to follow him as he walked laboriously to his front door. "Well that's fine, I've got a whole lot of pot roast needs eaten, and a comfy couch for you to crash on."

Bash shook his head, chuckled, and followed the man inside.

***

# From the Message Boards

## Topic: Black eyed kids in my neighborhood?!!

**Mrs.TomWilt** *9-12-1999 7:17pm*
I think I have black eyed kids on my street! They're always in groups of three or more, wearing hoodies, carrying skateboards. And the laughing! It's chilling. I've tried to call the police on them, but nothing has been done.

**Mrs.TomWilt** *9-12-1999 7:46pm*
They're out there right now, skateboarding around the cul de sac! What should I do??

**Raccoon** *9-12-1999 8:03pm*
Chill out, lady. Those are called teenagers.
***

Williams woke the next morning to find the couch empty, but there was a note left on the dining table.

Had to catch an early train.
Thank you.
-B

Williams folded the note, tucking it in a book he had on the counter. He put on a pot of coffee, the full twelve cups, then stepped onto his porch to grab the morning paper. The date read Saturday, April 15, 2000. Next weekend was Easter, and then a few weeks after that, he was supposed to show up at the VFW Hall for a ceremony. He was the only living WWII veteran in the tri-county area, and they were going to trot him out with medals and salutes and a band or something. He wasn't sure, but he knew there was a free meal in it for him, so he agreed to it. He stood and went to the whiteboard on the fridge. He erased, "Get eggs, dummy" and replaced it with, "Dry Clean Uniform."

The front door opened and the joyous cacophony of grandchildren poured in, followed by his son and daughter-in-law. "Hey Dad," he said. "We're the first this weekend?" His son set a paper bag on the table and began unloading it, breakfast casserole with sausage and potato, and a box of donuts.

Williams nodded. "Means you get the fresh coffee and the best donuts," he said and smiled.

# CHAPTER FOURTEEN

"More coffee?"

Cole looked up from his notes, blinking to focus on the waitress behind the counter. "Yeah, please," he said giving her a quick smile before he turned back to his work. It was eight in the morning. Cole hadn't slept much over the past few days, and it was starting to take its toll. A headache built of fatigue was winding its way through his brain, making it difficult to focus.

An ID had come back on one of the victims - Angel Rodriguez, a Desert Storm vet that had fallen through the cracks when he came home with PTSD. The female victim hadn't been identified - but Cole had a hunch that she was a runaway out of one of the larger cities nearby. Probably no older than twenty.

The homeless population was predictably unhelpful, though one of them had mumbled about aliens with big black eyes. While Cole wasn't about to start believing that these were alien abductions, the black-eyed children were beginning to seem more feasible. Coffee roiled in his stomach and he pushed away his plate of half-eaten eggs and bacon before dropping a $20 on the counter and nodding at the waitress.

Ten minutes later Cole was on Julia's welcome mat when Devin answered the door.

"Must be the changing of the guard," Devin said with a lazy smile. The taller man was wearing his jacket.

"Leaving?" Cole asked.

Devin nodded. "Work beckons, so Jules is on her own with her roommate interview today."

"How'd that go yesterday?" Cole stepped into the kitchen. He could hear the shower running at the end of the hall.

"Abysmally," Devin said. "You know, Dishy - *you* could always move in here. It would make this somewhat-awkward courtship you two have brewing far more interesting for me."

Cole blinked. "I'm not-" he paused. "There's no courtship, awkward or otherwise."

Devin put a hand on his shoulder, squeezing. "Sure." He waved and slipped out the door.

Cole was still standing in the kitchen, now acutely aware of how awkward he may or may not be when Julia came down the hall. She wore jeans and a t-shirt, and her wet hair was unbrushed and pulled into a clip at the back of her head. She smiled when she saw him.

"I'm assuming Devin let you in and that you aren't taking this stalking thing to a new level?" She slid past him to the coffee maker, frowning at the nearly empty pot before resetting the machine. "Devin drank all my coffee, but I'll have more in a minute if you want a cup."

"Thank you, but I can't stay long. I just wanted to check in and see if you were doing better."

"I am." She flipped the on switch on the coffee maker, then jumped up to sit on the counter next to it. "I think I'll be fine here alone tonight unless by some miracle my new perfect roommate comes walking through the door today." She glanced over at the front door and sighed. "I'm not holding my breath for that."

"I can come check on you tonight. I- I mean," he stuttered, Devin's words floating back through Cole's mind as he felt himself slipping precariously close to awkward. He stood straight, shaking himself. "If you feel it's necessary."

"As much as I enjoy your company, appreciate your concern, and plan on grilling you for on-the-record information in the very near future so I don't get fired," she hopped down off the counter and spun around to grab a mug from the cabinet and fill it with the last of the coffee, "I can't rely on you guys to keep me company until the end of time." She sipped the coffee black, wincing slightly at the heat. "I've been through traumatic shit before and came out mostly unscathed, barring a slight drinking problem and an aversion to children. I'll be fine."

Cole chuckled, shaking his head. "Well, you know how to reach me if you need anything."

"I do," she said and gestured to a cork board near the front door. Two of his cards were tacked to it.

"Okay, then," he nodded and turned for the door. "Take care, Julia."

"Hey, Cole?" She had set down her coffee and pulled on the arm of his jacket to turn him around before he reached the door. "I really do appreciate everything you've done for me the last few days." She stood on her tiptoes and kissed him quickly on the cheek before stepping lightly back to her cup of coffee. "And I really do mean it that I'm going to grill you about this case. Very soon."

"I'm sorry, Miss Winters," he said opening the door. "I'm not at liberty to discuss any information about this case with the press." He stepped through, hearing her amused voice follow him out as the door closed.

"That's a bunch of bullshit, Detective."

He hunched down in his coat, pulling it closed around his neck as he hurried down the sidewalk. The ritual wasn't working, and that made them angry. Their voices spoke in soft, low tones, hot knives slicing through his mind.

*"They need to know each other for it to work,"* said one.

*"They need to love each other for it to work,"* said the other.

*"So we can go home,"* they said together.

"I'm sorry," he said aloud, then looked around to make sure no one was within earshot. He lowered his voice to a whisper. "I'm sorry. I didn't know." He had one more block to walk, and the rain was starting to fall. He pulled his laptop bag closer, stuffing it under his arm. "I will try again."

*"Soon,"* they hissed in his mind. He flinched and ran the rest of the way down the block as the rain began to pour in earnest.

# CHAPTER FIFTEEN

"They're killing us, boss."

Devin choked on his bummed cigarette. "Jerry! You've really got to work on your greetings." He peeked out from under the awning, squinting through the rain into the alley and saw the old man, what was left of his white hair was plastered to his skull under an ineffective old leather hat. "Jesus, Jerry, come inside and get dry." He snuffed out the cigarette regretfully, then opened the door for the old man, waiting impatiently as he rolled his wheelchair through.

"Now what do you mean?" Devin took his coat off and hung it up on the hook behind the counter. "Who's killing whom?" He grabbed a fresh roll of paper towel and handed it to Jerry, shrugging when the man just stared at it.

"Them kids," the old man said. "They're taking us and killing us."

Devin's heart started to creep up his throat, but he swallowed it down. "You've seen them?"

The old man met Devin's eyes then, a clear, lucid, and

terrified crystal blue gaze beneath all the wrinkles and rags. "I've seen them, and they're going to take me, too."

The sharp ringing of his cell phone woke Cole from a restless sleep. He reached up, feeling around on the coffee table for the offending noise, flipping the phone open more to quiet it than to answer it. He brought it to his ear and stifled a yawn before saying, "Hello?"

"Heya, Dishy. I've got a friend in my shop that seems to think he's in danger."

"Devin?" Cole pulled himself to a sitting position, running a hand back through hair that probably needed a good shampoo.

"Yeah," said the voice on the other end of the line. "My friend Jerry is here saying that those creepy kids took some of his friends." Cole heard a muffled voice beyond Devin. "Sorry, not friends. Fellow street people." The muffled voice again, angrier this time. Devin's voice was faint when he spoke again, as though he'd put his hand over the receiver. "Do you live on the street, Jer? Yes? Then 'street person' applies in this scenario, doesn't it? That's right." A beat of silence and then Devin's voice came in clear again. "He's afraid, Detective."

Cole pulled his shirt from the back of the couch, sliding it over his arms. "I'll be there in ten," he said and hung up the phone.

Devin looked up from the counter with relief as Cole came in, shaking rain from his coat. He had given up trying to get info from Jerry, hoping the detective had some magical interrogation method for crazy homeless people.

"Did I wake you, or do you always look like that?" he asked Cole.

Cole looked up, running a hand back through his hair

in a failed attempt to tame it. "Both?" He squared his shoulders. "Where is your friend?"

Devin gestured for Cole to follow him around the counter and through an open archway to the storage room. Jerry was tucked in the corner next to a stack of copy paper, mumbling to himself. "Jer, this is my friend the detective. Think you can talk to him a little? He's here to help you, okay?"

A glimmer of lucidity shaded the old man's eyes as he looked up at Devin, and then Cole. "Two dead, aren't they?"

Cole crouched down in front of Jerry. "Yeah," he said. "Yeah, they are. Did you know them?"

Jerry nodded. "Little. Mexican and a new girl."

"Did you see what happened to them?" Cole asked. He reached for his notebook, but paused, not wanting to distract the man.

"Couple of kids - I saw them take the new girl." He gave Cole a long look. "I know she was new because she was on that corner all alone. She didn't have anyone else with her like you're supposed to in those situations." He paused, and Cole waited patiently. "Them kids came outta nowhere, swooped in and forced her into a blue car. I didn't even know they were there, and neither did she, I guess." A tear formed at the corner of the old man's eye. "Nothin' I could have done, you see?"

Cole put a hand on the man's shoulder. "That's true. You couldn't have helped. It's not your fault."

The tear slipped down Jerry's cheek, making a muddy trail.

"Can you remember anything else about the car? You said it was blue. Was it newer, do you think?"

Jerry shrugged. "Just a car, officer," he said. "Corner of First and Franklin. Not a corner you want to be at alone if you're a young lady..."

Cole stood, feeling that Jerry was fading again, and wanting to write down the information he did get. "Thank you, Jerry. If you think of anything else, please have Devin call me, okay?"

The old man didn't respond. Cole sighed and started to follow Devin back out to the front of the store when Jerry spoke up again, his voice shrill. "They're gonna come for all of us, boss, and they're gonna kill us."

Devin met Cole's eyes, a mixture of pity and fear written in his gaze. "I can keep him here during the day, but he can't be in here at night without supervision," Devin said in a low voice as they headed back out to the front of the store. "And as much as I love the guy, I don't know that my apartment is appropriate seeing as how it's a second-floor walk-up."

Cole nodded. "I can let him overnight in the drunk tank for a few days, but I'm not sure how comfortable he'll be."

Devin cleared his throat. "Then I guess you're just going to have to catch these little bastards soon, right?"

Cole ran a hand down his face, feeling the stubble of a few days neglect on his cheeks. "I guess so."

At nine that evening Julia was curled up on the couch in her softest, ugliest pajama pants, snuggling with a wooden bat as though it were her favorite teddy bear. The bat, it had belonged to her brother, was old and worn and the wood was soft to the touch. It was her security now that she'd insisted to both Cole and Devin that she could stay by herself in her own home for the night. She was surprised by how much comfort it gave her to have it nearby, and she wondered if just any old bat would have done that, or if it was the connection to her big brother that made her feel safe.

The dry drone of the television, some PBS

documentary, mixed with a heavy and persistent rain outside was lulling her into a light doze that she hoped might convert to a sleep that would last until morning. She was just drifting off when there was a knock at her door. She was on her feet before she was fully awake, heart pounding, fist clenched around the handle of the bat. She tiptoed to the door, putting her hand on it. "Who is it?"

A voice, vaguely familiar reached through the door. "It's Bash."

Julia frowned. "Bash?" Her hand reflexively tightened around the bat. "What are you doing here? How do you know where I live?"

"Phone directory, Julia Winters," he drawled. "And I'm here because I think we can help each other."

Julia scoffed. "How's that?"

"All right, look, I walked here from the train station, and it ain't getting any warmer and drier out here. What say you open the door and let me in?"

Julia closed her eyes and took a deep breath. "Okay," she whispered and opened the door.

Bash was soaked to the skin, hair and clothes dripping onto the welcome mat. He should have looked like a drowned rat, but he lounged somehow - hands in his pockets and his face pulled into a smirk as he looked her up and down.

"Nice pants," he said.

"They were a gift. And they're comfortable," she said defensively. She lifted the bat. "What the hell do you want?"

He put his hands in front of him, posture diminishing slightly. "Sorry. I'm sorry." He looked down. "It's just that they're very... bright."

Julia scowled. "Goodbye, Bash." She swung the door closed, but he blocked it with an outstretched hand.

"No. Damnit, okay," he shifted again, now beginning to look a little more pathetic, though not losing enough of that palpable confidence to convince Julia it was real. "I really am sorry. Give me a chance?"

He set her on edge, but that could be because he had leaped artfully over every question she'd asked the last time she saw him.

She was still undecided when the phone rang behind her, and she turned, leaving the door open for him. He stepped in and closed it, trailing a puddle of mud and rain onto her kitchen floor. She picked up her phone, turning away from him again. "Hello?"

"Look Julia. I know you've had a rough week, but the press does not take a mental health day."

Julia grimaced. "Good evening, Mrs. Hall. I know, and I am very sorry about that."

"You should be, Julia. Bradley doesn't appear to have the tenacity you do. Some horrible cop told him to leave the scene of a crime, and do you know what he did?"

Julia sat silent for a moment.

"He *left* the *scene* of the *crime*! Without any good photos or statements or anything!"

Julia stifled the laughter that threatened to bubble up. "I'm very sorry, Mrs. Hall."

"Yes, well," her editor said. "His father was equally as effective in all things… Anyway, there's a story over at the high school. Nothing exciting, just a little fluffy piece about one of the teachers taking underprivileged kids to ball games or something. I already sent Chandra up to interview the guy, I just need a few pictures to go with it."

Julia grabbed a notepad and pencil and jotted down the name of the teacher. "Okay, I'll head there first thing in the morning."

"That's good, Julia," her editor said. "I'm taking it

easy on you now, but I want you up and getting me front page news again soon, do you understand?"

"Yes, Mrs. Hall."

"Good," she said and hung up the phone.

"Look," Julia turned back to face Bash. "I've got an early morning, so I don't have time for-" She broke off mid-sentence mouth falling open slightly.

It wasn't the growing puddle at his feet that was starting to stain her carpet, nor the fact that this was the first time she'd seen him in proper lighting that proved her suspicions that he was really quite attractive. It was Rufus.

The cat was on the kitchen counter, chirping at Bash as he spun around and pushed himself into Bash's hands repeatedly. Rufus, who still tried to attack even Devin whom he had known since Julia had brought him home, was trying to climb up the front of this stranger's soaking wet jacket, purring. Bash was smiling, the smirk gone as he focused on the little bundle of normally-angry fluff.

Julia shook her head and plopped down on a stool at the counter. "Okay," she set the bat down. "Talk."

He pulled off his pack, setting it on the ground, then took a seat, allowing the cat to find its way to his lap and curl up. "I've decided to stay in town for a while. Your friend said you needed a roommate. I need a place to stay. Seems like we could help each other."

She blinked. "Where are you from?"

His head cocked to the side, and he studied her for a moment before answering. "Tennessee."

She frowned. "You don't sound like you're from Tennessee."

"I haven't been back in a very long time."

"What were you doing by the warehouse district the night we met?"

"The night I saved you?"

Julia set her jaw. She stood, rounding the counter and pulling a fifth of whiskey from the cupboard, along with two glasses. She set them on the counter between them, pouring two fingers into each. "Yes," she said, settling down in her chair again and taking a sip of her drink. "That night."

"I told you, I had just hopped off the train." He took the glass, swirling the thick liquid.

"And I told you, trains don't run on that track any longer."

Bash shrugged. "This one did."

Julia closed her eyes, taking a deep breath before she downed the rest of her drink and poured herself another. "Why did you come here, to Grand River?"

"The train stopped."

"Where were you before here?"

He smirked, "Am I being interrogated? Are you a cop?"

"Journalist," she said. "And yes - it's the potential roommate interview."

"I got on the train in a tiny town I guarantee you've never heard of. I like to read the newspaper, I can cook a mean stew, and I've been a lot of places before I was here." He sipped his whiskey. "Do I get to ask you some questions as well?" Julia crossed her arms over her chest. "No questions from me, then." He paused. "Except…"

"What?"

"What's the cat's name?" He lifted the purring creature out of his lap, setting him on the counter where he pouted for a moment before Bash continued petting.

"Rufus." Julia studied the two of them. The cat curling up on the counter and closing his eyes. Bash had his gaze on the cat, but Julia got the distinct impression that his focus was elsewhere. He was still damp, small droplets of water gathered in his hair. He wore a simple

126

leather jacket, brand new by the looks of it, the pleasant smell of it had been on the periphery of her senses. All of his clothes looked somewhat new. Her memory flashed back to the first night she met him, dirty and bedraggled, as he searched the Knox kid's pockets for a pack of smokes and a lighter. She narrowed her eyes at him.

"Did you steal that guy's wallet?" Bash looked up brows drawing together in puzzlement. "The guy that was there with me that night in the warehouse."

He smirked. "Rescue fee."

"Are you going to steal from me?" She waited, chewing her lip as he studied her.

"Probably not."

She held his gaze for a long moment, searching for the reason that her gut was telling her to let him stay, despite her better judgment yelling that she should chase him out with her brother's bat. His eyes were clear and sharp, and he met her silent gaze with a snake-like stillness.

"How old are you?" she asked.

"Older than I look." He leaned back in his seat. "Mind if I smoke?"

She stood, taking the fifth and pouring herself one more drink before walking around the counter and putting it back on its shelf. "Only in your room, and only with the window open and the fan pointing out." She downed the alcohol in one gulp, feeling it roil in her stomach almost immediately. "First door on the right. There's a bed with sheets and a blanket you can use, and a nightstand with a lamp and a fan. Rent is $200 and it's due this week, and then on the first of the month from then on out." She turned to face him, pleased to see that he was slightly surprised. "Electric, cable, and phone are split 50/50. You're welcome to use the computer, just don't go to any dodgy sites that'll jack it up with a virus or something." He looked confused for a brief moment but shook it off as his eyes tracked her across the apartment.

She stopped at the door to her room, opening it and looking back at him. "My room is off limits unless you legitimately believe I am dying. And even then, knock repeatedly first." She turned in the doorway. He still sat at the counter, Rufus tucked into the crook of his arm fast asleep. "Lock the door before you turn in. Good night, Bash."

His voice traveled down the hall, reaching her just as she shut her door. "G'night, Winters."

\*\*\*

# From the Message Boards

## Topic: Oregon BEK Near Miss

**Forgotten1968**  *3-5-2000, 5:59pm*
If you knew what you'd given up…

**Raccoon**  *3-5-2000, 6:34pm*
This is getting old.

**DiabloMaster**  *3-22-2000, 1:46am*
METALLICA SUX!!!

\*\*\*

Bash sat at the counter in what was now his apartment and nursed his glass of whiskey. Since getting off the train he had still been a bit of a transient, and he'd been able to tuck away the oddness of this world by holding onto that fact. Now he was … stationary. Tonight he would sleep in his own bed, not cot, not sleeping bag, not discarded tattered mattress, but an actual bed. His eyes strayed to the door, feeling the heaviness of his pack leaning against his foot.

*Out the door, into a cab and be out of town and on another train in an hour...*

Rufus stirred in his sleep, poking his head under Bash's palm. Reflexively he ran his hand over the cat's head and was rewarded with a half-asleep purr. His eyes strayed down the hall to the door the Winters girl had disappeared through twenty minutes earlier. The cat liked him more than she did. But that didn't matter much, he just wanted to make sure these black-eyed bastards were done messing with her.

*Why do you care? Grab the bag, steal a car, get the hell out of town...*

He shifted in his seat, taking a look around at the apartment. It was simple, but not plain. Framed photos of the river and the lake hung on the walls. The furniture didn't match but looked homey and comfortable. It wasn't clean, but it wasn't dirty, and definitely better than living in the old, abandoned service station that had been his last semi-permanent residence. The bat that Julia had been wielding when she answered the door was resting against her empty chair.

*She can obviously take care of herself...*

Bash stood, pulling the backpack onto one shoulder and patted the disgruntled cat on the head. "Sorry, cat. I think it's best if I jet," he said quietly before taking the few short steps to the door. His hand was on the doorknob, when he paused, eyes focusing on a corkboard next to the door frame. A few business cards, a few notes to and from the previous roommate, and a picture. White framed and faded, there were four figures in the photo. A woman who he took for Julia at first, but she was a little older and a little softer around the edges upon closer inspection. A little blond girl with pigtails that couldn't have been more than seven years old. A man who was obviously her father, one hand resting on her shoulder while the other was wrapped around his wife's waist. The girl was looking at the boy next to her, tall and gangly and heading into his awkward years. He was looking back at the girl with a grin, sharing a joke when the photo was taken. A tiny spark in his long memory flashed to life and he saw that boy, maybe a couple years older, standing in front of him bruised, defiant, and needing help.

*Gene… goddamnit.*

He took his hand off the doorknob, reaching up to turn the lock on the deadbolt instead before sighing and turning to face the apartment. Rufus looked at him expectantly. "Yeah, I know," he said to the cat. He pushed himself away from the front door and headed down the hall to his room, the backpack falling from his shoulder and into his hand.

*Damnit.*

# CHAPTER SIXTEEN

"Did you even go home last night, detective?"

Cole looked up from his desk to see Sargent Biggs peeking over the wall of his cubicle. She disappeared for a moment before reappearing around the side of the wall, hanging her coat on the coat rack.

"Yeah, for a couple hours," Cole answered. "Couldn't really sleep, though - so I figured I'd come back and try to do some work."

"Get anywhere?" she asked.

"Not in the slightest," Cole mumbled, scanning the papers on his desk. "This came in for you on the fax, though." He picked up a small stack of papers and handed them to her.

She flipped through them. "They found that stolen rental," she said. "Abandoned at a Whataburger in Kansas." She flipped another couple pages and vanished out of sight again. He heard her at her desk near the front door as she picked up the phone and called the contact on the cover sheet.

Cole turned back to his work, tuning out the phone

call chatter. The homeless victims both had head injuries, much like Julia and Tim Knox had sustained. The girl had died first, slow exsanguination. Mr. Rodriguez had been alive when they slit his throat. No matter how many times he rehashed it, revulsion churned his stomach when he thought of their fate. No prints left at the newest scene. Nothing to go on apart from the witness account of a half-crazy homeless man.

The front door opened. Cole cocked his head, listening to Biggs finish her conversation and hang up the phone before she said, "Hi, can I help you?"

"Hey, I'm here for my buddy Jerry," said another voice. "Old guy, kinda dusty. On wheels."

Cole stood, spying the top of Devin's head over the cubicle wall. "I've got this, Sargent," he said.

Devin turned and offered a bright smile. "Good morning, Dishy!"

Cole grit his teeth as he saw Biggs' face break into a grin. He cleared his throat, "Sargent Biggs, this is Devin."

Devin turned to the officer and offered his hand. "Hi. My best friend was almost barbecued the other day."

Biggs shook his hand. "Oh, the young woman? How is she?"

"Drinking a lot and carrying a bat around," Devin put his hands in the pockets of his wool coat, "so almost back to normal."

Biggs chuckled, "My kinda girl."

"Mine too," Devin said.

"Come on back and we'll get Jerry," Cole motioned to Devin and headed toward a door at the back of the room. The taller man followed into a dimly lit hallway.

"So," Devin said. "How's everything going?"

Cole let out a tired laugh. "You mean, have I found the killers yet?"

"Yeah, basically."

"Unfortunately, no," Cole said. They turned a corner and faced a locked, barred door. "I can't seem to figure out where the local demon teens hang out."

Devin stopped, turning toward Cole. "Wait, demon teens? Do you honestly believe there's something X-Filesian going on?" He studied Cole for a moment.

"What about Julia-"

Devin put a hand on Cole's shoulder. "Julia knows full well I think she's 85% batshit crazy when it comes to this stuff. Sure, my fight or flight has been running pretty high when I see a group of kids in hooded sweatshirts the last few days, but that's all they are, kids."

"You have a very good point," Cole said, laughing softly.

Devin followed him down another short hall to the holding cells. "You're not the first guy to get all caught up in a distressed damsel's story." He patted the detective on the back then turned to look into the dim cell. "Jerry, my good man! Let's get out of here and get you some coffee and breakfast pie."

Cole opened the cell and let Devin wheel the old man back down the hall and to the front office. He waved to Biggs on the way out, thanking her for the hospitality on Jerry's behalf. The old man smiled at them and lifted his hand, mumbling something about pie.

Cole went back to his desk, looking down at the nest of papers.

Out of the corner of his eye, he saw Biggs in the doorway, arms folded across her chest. "So," she said, voice a deceptive sing-song. "What are you planning for the day, Dishy?"

Julia's alarm went off at 6:30 am. She smacked the top of the clock, then stretched, feeling muscles strain against the movement. She was still sore from her struggles against the ropes, but getting better. The burn on her cheek had all but disappeared, and the bump on her head was nearly gone and just a little tender. She yawned and sat up, putting her feet on the wood floor. She felt rested for the first time in days but got a jolt of discomfort, when events of the previous night rushed back to her.

Bash was here. Unless he'd left in the night with all her valuables. Or her cat.

She grabbed a bathrobe to protect against the morning chill and quietly opened her door. The door across the hall into the spare room was closed. The light from the television cast shadows at the end of the hall. Everything was silent. She tiptoed to the living room. Bash's coat was draped over the chair he'd sat in last night. The door was locked from the inside. Nothing appeared to be missing.

She picked up the bat she'd left leaning against the counter and put it back in the closet. She took the beer bottles from the coffee table and the glasses that had been left on the counter and deposited them in the sink. A brochure under Bash's chair caught her eye and she picked it up, opening it without thinking. Inside was a train ticket from Lawrence, Kansas to Grand River, Michigan. She closed it and stuffed it lightly back into the pocket of his jacket. The urge to see if she could make anything else accidentally fall from the pockets was strong, but she shook away the temptation and put on coffee instead. She was due at the school in a half hour, there would be time for spying on her new roommate later.

Bash was in and out of sleep when he heard Julia getting ready. Rufus the cat snuggled in next to him was an odd comfort that kept pulling him back into half dreams. It wasn't until he heard the heavy front door close and lock that he sat up, displacing the cat. Rufus scowled at him, then ran to the door, chirping at him.

"Right," he mumbled, running a hand back through his hair. He opened the door, peeking out to make sure no one was there before wandering into the hall behind the cat. Rufus ran into the kitchen, finding newly poured food and water left under the counter. Bash followed, finding a note and a key waiting for him.

*The coffee is fresh but might need a reheat depending on how long you sleep. Here's a key in case you leave before I come back. Do not forget to lock the door behind you. Help yourself to what's in the fridge for breakfast - we can work out groceries later.*
*-Julia*

Well, succinct wasn't necessarily unfriendly, and she hadn't told him to get out, so that was promising. He poured himself a cup of coffee and wondered how long she'd be gone. He found himself with not a lot to do for the first time in … what could easily be construed as forever … and he wasn't quite sure what to do with that. A shower and a shave would probably be a good start. Then maybe devote some time to the television, see if he can glean a little more information about the world around him. Maybe pet the cat some more.

The possibilities were endless.

Grand River High School, home of the Rascals, had been brand new in the sixties when Julia's parents had attended. Nearly thirty years later when Julia graduated it had begun to show some wear and tear. Rebuild projects popped up every season with each new millage. There was a new wing with a brand new art department, and the parking lot had been recently repaved. The awning above the main entrance had been redone and stood proudly blue and shiny silver against the morning sun.

Julia ducked under the awning and let herself into the breezeway. The familiar smell of high school sent her temporarily back in time. Her aunt, her mother's sister, had taken custody of her after her father had been murdered and Gene kidnapped. Under the advisement of her psychologists, her aunt had grudgingly moved to Grand River to raise Julia in familiar territory. So Julia had been able to walk the same halls, and in some cases, even have the same teachers as her parents had. As soon as Julia graduated, her aunt tried to move them to Ann Arbor, a much larger college town on the other side of the state. Julia allowed it, but only long enough to obtain a degree from a two-year photojournalism course. Her aunt never understood Julia's pull to Grand River - and Julia was never able to explain it. Here she was close to her family, even if they were silent ghosts in her mind, walking the halls of the high school, buried in the small cemetery on the north side of town, or haunting the broken down arcade in the strip mall. They were still here for her, and so she would never leave.

"Miss Winters?"

Julia started, realizing she'd been drawn into the glass case in the entryway that held the old class photos. Not for the first time, she'd scanned the faces until she found first her mother, then her father, in the class of 1970. Tiny sepia-toned faces that had only just started dating each other and hadn't even thought about what they would name their future children. Though her father always insisted that as soon as he saw her he knew they would have a boy and a girl and live happily ever after.

"Julia?"

She turned, swallowing the bittersweet, and offered a smile to the white-haired man standing in the office doorway. "Principal Underhill," she said. "Good morning."

"Good morning, Miss Winters." He stepped out of the office, using a cane to hobble over to her. His knees had begun to deteriorate when she was in school, and she frowned to see him moving so slow now. "What can I do for you?"

"Well first you can get yourself some new knees, Mr. Underhill," she said. She met him halfway and gave him a warm hug. "You deserve it, sir."

The older man chuckled. "I keep asking Santa, but he has yet to deliver." He hugged her back, then stood up, eyeing her. "Are you here to take over for the art teacher? Because I will fire that old bat right now if you are."

Julia smiled and shook her head. "Boss sent me to get a photo of your new counselor, and maybe some of the kids he's mentoring."

The principal hung his head in mock sadness. "A shame, truly. You let me know when you come to your senses and want a real job, young lady."

"You let me know when you come to your senses and get some new knees, old man."

Mr. Underhill scowled at her and pointed his cane down the hall on the left. "Mr. Hudson is in Mrs. Shafer's old office - I trust you remember?"

"Of course," she said, and nodded a goodbye to the older man before heading down to her old counselor's office. Mrs. Shafer had retired the year before. Julia had run into her often at the library and had pleasant conversations with the old woman who probably knew more about her and her family than most people ever would. She had been the counselor for the entire school, elementary through high school, so she had already been helping Julia cope, even before the Disneyland trip.

There was a middle-aged man with sandy hair at her desk now, an open file in front of him. He looked up when she knocked on the door frame. "Mr. Hudson?"

He looked startled, seeing her, then shook himself and stood, coming around the desk to offer a hand. "You're the photographer from the paper?"

"Yes," she said, shaking his hand. "Julia Winters. Nice to meet you. I hear you're doing some great things with the kids here."

"That's what I hope," he said. "Come on in and have a seat."

Julia hesitated, feeling strange in this office after so many years, with a stranger behind that desk. "I don't want to take up too much of your time this morning, Mr. Hudson-"

"You can call me Patrick, Julia," he said.

She bit back a frown. "Patrick, where would you like to do the photos for the paper? And did you want me to include any of the students that you're working with?"

He shrugged, putting his hands in his pockets. "I'm sure we could pull a couple from class. Where would you suggest we do the photo?"

"Well, what kind of projects have you and the kids done? Is there something here at the school?"

He grimaced. "Not really, most of the stuff we do is outside of the school, community work and the like."

"Well, we could just shoot out in front, by the Rascals logo. It's not too cold this morning."

The man smiled, "That sounds perfect. I'll gather a few students and meet you out there in ten minutes?"

Julia nodded and left his office.

Cole didn't grow up in Grand River. The detective position had brought him to town six years earlier, but walking into Grand River High with the universal smell of chalk dust and textbooks thick in the air was a brief but strong hit of nostalgia. He quickly brushed the feeling aside, avoiding any unwanted memories. He heard sharp footfalls coming down the hall to his right, halting suddenly as they came into the school lobby.

"You're taking this stalking thing to a whole new level."

Cole looked up, surprised. Julia stood there looking at him with confusion and possibly a little annoyance. He put his hands up, "I swear to you, I didn't know you were here." He pulled the pinky and thumb in on his right hand so three fingers stood out. "Scouts honor."

She studied him for a moment, then relaxed. "I'm sorry," she said. "You just startled me. What are you doing here?"

He sighed, rubbing his eyes. The lack of sleep was starting to catch up to him. "I stopped here first after Tim Knox was taken. Just realized I should probably do some follow up interviews since so much has happened since then."

Julia nodded. "Makes sense."

"Hey, I meant to check in on you last night, but by the time I was done sorting Devin's friend Jerry it was really late and I didn't want to wake you."

"Jerry?" she said, brows drawn. "Is he okay?"

"Yeah, he's okay. He just seems to have witnessed one of the kidnappings, and he's understandably distressed." He scratched his head. "Did you manage okay alone last night?"

"Yeah," Julia said quickly. "Actually I got a roommate. But I was good either way." She nodded. "Definitely feeling a little less freaked out about things."

"A roommate?"

"Yeah," she looked down into her camera bag, pulling out her digital camera. "I've gotta go get set up for this shoot, but we can chat later if that's okay?" She grinned at him. "I have many questions about the case you're working on, Detective." She began to walk away, but paused, turning back to him. "Oh hey, Tim Knox and his dad, are they recovering well?"

Cole narrowed his eyes at her. "Press is still not allowed bother them in the hospital."

"Detective!" she scolded. "I'm not the press, I saved that boy's life! I'm invested."

Cole tried to frown, but he turned away quickly, so she didn't see the smile cracking through. "Go to work, Julia."

Hot showers were quickly becoming one of Bash's favorite perks of this world. He leaned his head down, letting the stream hit the back of his neck and shoulders, finding muscles that had been tight so long they might never be fully relaxed again. He could have stayed there all morning, but he felt his ears twitch, honing in on sounds that didn't make sense in an empty apartment.

Without turning off the water, he stepped out and onto the fuzzy grey bath mat and grabbed a towel from the shelf, wrapping it securely around his waist. He put his ear to the door, blocking out the sound of the shower. He could hear footsteps in the kitchen, and the fridge opening. A cleared throat told him it was a man, and not Julia. He glanced around but didn't see anything that might be weapon worthy. He'd be damned if he showed up to a potential fight with a hot pink hairbrush and lavender shampoo.

He eased the door open, turning the knob silently and opening it a crack to peek through. Whoever was in the kitchen was out of his line of sight. He slipped through the door and padded quickly down the hall, pressing his back against the wall. He peeked around the corner and felt the breath he was holding rush out in a silent laugh. Julia's friend Devin was in her kitchen, head stuck in the fridge.

"Good morning," he said, and held back more laughter as the man jumped, stumbling backward. "How can I help you?"

He recovered quickly and stood, straightening his coat. "Um. Hi." He offered a somewhat uncomfortable smile and cocked his head to look around Bash toward the bathroom where the shower was still running. "Is Julia here?"

Bash shook his head. "No, she left early this morning." He crossed his arms over his chest and leaned his shoulder against the wall. "Is there something you needed?"

"No," Devin said. "I just brought her some breakfast. It's in the fridge if she wants it when she gets back."

"Okay," Bash said. "You're welcome to stay till she gets back."

Devin wound his way around the counter and toward the front door. "No, I've got a senile homeless man in my car. But thanks. I'll just catch up to her later." He put his hand on the door, then turned back to Bash. "Um. Bye." He gave an awkward wave and disappeared through the door, locking it with a key from the outside.

Bash suppressed a shiver, damp skin making the room feel colder than it really was. He turned, eyeing the warm steam pouring out of the half-open bathroom door before deciding he wasn't quite done with his shower.

A lighting kit wasn't totally necessary with the current natural lighting, but it had been expensive and it looked fancy, so Julia set it up anyway. Two softboxes on either side of the Rascals sign would light a small group evenly. She clicked her shutter, testing the receivers to make sure the strobes worked. She was blinking away the afterimages when she felt her pager buzz and looked to see Devin's number followed by "911." She made her way to the lone pay phone in the breezeway between the lobby and the outside and dropped in a quarter. He answered on the second ring.

"Julia?" he asked.

"Hey," she said. "Everything okay?"

"Everything's fine…" he let the silence hang for a moment. "Oh, hey, were you aware that there's a half-naked transient in your apartment this morning?"

Julia rolled her eyes. "You're the one who suggested he move in with me."

"I cannot be blamed for anything I say pre-karaoke." He paused again. "Did you…?"

"What?" Julia felt her face flush. "No, of course not. He needs a place to live, I need a roommate, it works out." She turned around, seeing an empty foyer behind her, she turned back and lowered her voice. "Plus, I feel like he knows something he's not telling me about these kids."

There was a long pause on the other end. "So, you've invited a mysterious homeless guy with secrets to live in your home. Hey, me too! We're starting a new trend."

Julia laughed. "How is Jerry?"

"Bats in the belfry, as per usual," he said.

"I'll be by after I'm done here - we can talk then, okay?"

They said their goodbyes and Julia hung up the phone. She turned and bit back a shriek as her eyes focused on four silent figures on the other side of the breezeway doors. They all turned as Patrick Hudson came up behind them, and Julia could see their faces. Just kids. General aura of teenaged unwillingness and a sullen expression in their completely normal eyes. Patrick opened the door and ushered them through, looking up at Julia as they passed. "Are we ready?"

"Certainly," she said and followed the group to the mascot sign. "Shouldn't take too long."

"I'm getting out of P.E., Lady," said one of the kids, a taller skinny boy. "Take as long as you want."

"You need P.E.," said another one, a girl this time. "You need muscles."

The taller boy put his arm around the girl in a mock headlock, the girl poked him in the ribs and he let her go, giggling.

Julia smiled. "So is this all of you?" She began positioning them around the sign.

Patrick spoke up, "Not at all. We've got quite a few kids in the program. These guys were just easy to find because they were hiding in the library pretending to study."

"I met Devin ditching class in the library," Julia laughed. She gestured to Patrick to join the teens, standing in the middle behind the Rascals sign. He leaned forward, putting his elbows on the top of the sign, and the kids squeezed in close on either side of him.

"Is Devin your husband?" Patrick asked.

"No, he's my best friend," Julia said. "Better than a husband if you ask me because if he annoys me, I can just go home." She clicked the shutter after she spoke, catching the group mid-laughter. She snapped a couple more before nodding. "I think we've got it. Your story will probably be in tomorrow's paper." She shook Mr. Hudson's hand, thanking him for his time before she started packing up her equipment.

Ten minutes later she was all packed up and heading to her car.

"How about lunch?"

She stopped and turned. Cole was coming out of the

double doors. He jogged over to her and took the heavy bag holding the lighting kit out of her hands.

"Lunch?" she asked. She continued to her car and he kept pace next to her.

"Burgers and day beers, I'm thinking. And some 'on the record' information about The Case of the Singed Photojournalist."

They stopped at her car. She unlocked it and looked up at him. "Some?"

He opened the back door and slid her lighting kit onto the seat. "Enough for a good story, but not so much that you blow my case while I'm still cracking it."

She tossed her camera bag onto the passenger seat, then turned around to face him, leaning on her car. "There will be *off* the record information as well, yes?"

"One o' clock at Charlie's?" he offered, avoiding the question.

She smiled. "See you there."

There was sand in Bash's shoes.

He'd tried to find something on the television after his shower, but having been met with nothing but chirping and false-bright morning talk shows, he decided that exploring his new hometown was a preferable option. The town map in the brochure he'd taken from the train station told him that there was a main street with a market district just a few blocks away from Julia's apartment complex. When he'd gotten there, his attention was drawn to a boardwalk that drew foot traffic from the market district, over a vast expanse of beach, and down to water and waves. He followed the boardwalk down a few hundred yards, but hopped off it into the sand before long, finding a place to stop just out of range of the highest waves lapping against the shore.

It was cold, the wind coming off the water chilled and

persistent. Bash took his shoes off, pouring them clean and setting them aside. The sand was damp from the overnight rain, it stuck to his bare feet and defied physics somehow, crawling up his ankles and onto his pants within seconds.

As a young man, he had spent a summer in his early teens wandering up the Atlantic coast, scamming tourists and sleeping where the waves lulled him to dreams and the watery sunrise woke him every morning. He took a few steps forward, gritting his teeth as the waves washed over his feet. It was the kind of cold that hurt, but it felt amazing. A shock of clarity reminding him that he was far, far away from his last home. It grounded him in the here and now more than he was particularly comfortable with, and he sighed, moving away from the water and back up the beach to continue his exploration.

"There she is," Devin said when Julia opened the door. "Hey Jerry, Jules is here," he yelled behind him toward the back room.

"Did she bring pie?" came a muffled voice.

"Not likely, Jer," Devin called back. He turned to Julia. "See, he's upset because I bought an extra slice of pie at breakfast and then dropped it off at your house instead of saving it for him. I explained to him that he doesn't need two pieces of pie in one morning, but he doesn't buy it. So tell me how you acquired your new hero transient roommate."

Julia blinked, brain processing her friend's quick speech a few seconds behind. "Good morning, Devin. I am well, and yourself?"

"I am well and curious, Jules," Devin said. He leaned his elbows on the counter. "Tell me."

She set her bag on the counter, pulling out the roll of film for processing and handed it to him. "Get that started and I'll tell you all the sultry details."

Devin took it and fiddled with it for a moment before feeding it into the processing machine. Then he turned back to Julia, leaning back against the machine and cocked a brow at her. "So?"

Julia sighed. "He showed up at my place. I interviewed him. We're trying out the roommate thing. There's nothing really out-of-the-ordinary about it."

"Except that he saved your life a few days ago."

"Well, then the least I could do is offer him a place to stay."

"And he's a self-professed transient."

"Well, then I will just have to find another roommate when he transients off in the near future."

"And how does the good detective feel about it?"

"I haven't told him…"

Devin crossed his arms in front of his chest. "Jules…."

"I'm not ready to share that information yet."

"Don't make me lie to Cole. Our relationship is young and fragile and cannot handle secrets."

"Just give me a little time."

"I don't know how I feel about it, Jules."

Julia sighed and hopped up on the counter. "To be honest, neither do I, Devin."


"Thank you for meeting with me, Mr. Hudson. Seems like you're pretty busy today." Cole sat across from the counselor and pulled his notebook from his coat.

"Not at all," Patrick Hudson said, nudging his chair forward to lean against his desk. "I'm feeling strangely popular today." The man smiled at Cole. "What can I do for you?"

"Principal Underhill suggested I talk to you. I'm looking into the recent incidents involving a group of kids."

"The fire, right?" Hudson said gravely. "I couldn't believe that happened in our little town. I'm just relieved that no one was seriously hurt."

The second incident, and subsequent deaths, had yet to hit the papers. The rumor mill was buzzing, but evidently, nothing had yet reached the man in front of him. "Yes, well. Have you seen anything you would consider suspicious among any groups of students? I know that a couple of them would have had injuries from the incident last week. Any unexplained black eyes, broken noses, or odd behavior?"

Hudson sighed. "Well, this is a high school. It's safe to say that all behavior is odd behavior at this age. As for injuries, we've got a few so-called 'bad apples' that are always getting into fights, so nothing stands out as unexpected."

Cole reached into his pocket and pulled out a business card as he stood. "I won't take up any more of your time today, then. If you remember anything, or if you do see anything that you feel is a concern, please give me a call."

The counselor stood and shook Cole's hand. "Of course, Detective."

A sharp ringing cut Cole's response off. He grabbed his phone out of his pocket and nodded to Mr. Hudson before leaving the office. He flipped the phone open, "This is Cole."

"Looks like my stolen car case might be your stolen car case, Cole." Sergeant Biggs sounded surprised.

"How's that?" Cole asked.

"The prints came back, and they match your wallet and knife prints. The old guy."

"No kidding?" Cole wound his way out the door of the school, waving at the secretary behind the desk in the front office before he left.

"Wish I was," Biggs sighed. "I told the local PD to keep an eye out for any strange old dudes. They laughed at me."

"Can't say I blame them." Cole chuckled.

"Now you're laughing at me," Biggs said. "This is *your* old guy, Cole. You should be the one getting razzed about it."

"Fair enough," Cole said. "I'll be back at the station shortly."

He could practically hear the grin through the phone. "Sounds good, Dishy."

"Julia!"

Julia forced a smile at her editor, bracing herself. "Hello, Mrs. Hall."

"It's so good to see you!" Mrs. Hall stood, coming around from her desk and putting her long, bony arms around Julia. "You look lovely for someone who was almost dead a few days ago."

Julia stifled a frown. "Thanks."

Mrs. Hall let her go and swept back into her desk chair. "Do you have my photos?" Julia reached into her bag and pulled out the prints and negatives from her shoot with the counselor. Mrs. Hall frowned. "You didn't use the digital?"

"No, Mrs. Hall," Julia said. "But I will bring it when I go out to the site of the second incident."

Mrs. Hall frowned. "Oh yes. The one that Bradley flubbed." She sighed heavily. "Stop by his office on your way out to get the location."

Julia nodded and began backing out of her editor's office. "Yes, Mrs. Hall. Thank you." She bumped into a shelf and turned to see a small stack of today's paper. She slid one off the top, rolling it and stuffing it into her bag.

"I'll send you the images as soon as I can. Have a great afternoon, Mrs. Hall."

The woman was busy holding the negatives up to the light, mumbling acknowledgment as Julia slipped out the door and down the hall toward Bradley's office.

He stared at his hands, vision blurring, trying and failing to block out the voices.

*"Her, we want her,"* one of them said.

*"She has a connection, she's the key,"* the other intoned.

*"We just want to go home,"* the first one said.

"I know," he said under his breath. He picked at a hangnail and shifted in his chair. "I'm almost ready. It's almost time. I just need a few more days."

*"The time is now,"* said the more feminine voice, peeling back a layer of brain matter and sending a shooting pain deep into his skull.

*"Get us home,"* said the other voice, tendrils of fire and ice licked around the imaginary wound in his head.

"Okay," he whimpered. He hunkered down in his chair, clutching at his head. "One day and it's done."

He heard footsteps in the hall toward his office and shook himself, sitting straight and tall and taking deep breaths to compose. The headache began to fade. He knew who they wanted, he just needed to find the place and get the kids together. One day was enough time.

# CHAPTER SEVENTEEN

Charlie's was a dive bar that sat just off the boardwalk with no windows to see the dazzling sunset over the lake. It had been a grungy, greasy, and delicious staple in the community since the late 1950s, and had passed hands from father to son twice since its inception.

Mitchell, Charlie's grandson, and his wife had taken the reins in the mid-nineties, appeasing the Community Development Board by installing a patio to attract tourists and offering child size sand pails full of long island iced tea during the summer months. Julia had had one all to herself on the night of her 21st birthday and had sworn off Triple Sec forever when she woke the next day.

Pete the bartender hadn't let her forget it, occasionally standing across from her at the bar while he mixed a pail up for some poor pre-regrets individual. He would pour the booze from high above the bucket, waiting until she turned slightly green at the smell, and then walk away giggling like no tall, brawny, bearded man should ever be allowed to giggle.

Pete was behind the bar when Julia walked in. He grinned and waved at her, and she returned the gesture before scanning the tables for Cole. She found him sitting along the wall in a dark booth with a pint of something amber in front of him. He was scribbling in his notebook, head bowed forward. He looked up when she sat across from him and smiled.

"Hi," he said. He sat straighter and tucked the notepad back in the pocket of his jacket. "How's it going?"

"Good," she said. "I'm good, actually. You?"

"Tired," he said.

"Understandably."

Pete appeared at the booth, setting a pint of cheap beer in front of her. "You guys eating?"

"Definitely," Cole said, looking past the burly man to the board of specials behind the bar.

They decided to split the Charlie's Special Pizza, a hand-tossed crust covered in tomato sauce, cheese blend, super spicy sausage and banana peppers.

"So we found more prints from the old guy," Cole said after Pete left the table. He finished off the beer in front of him. "On a car that was stolen from the hotel here, and found in Kansas."

"You're kidding me," Julia said. In the back of her mind, a puzzle piece stood at attention.

"Nope," Cole said. "He's an old guy on the move."

Julia smiled, trying to shake the puzzle piece that was now jittering against her conscious mind.

"He's a suspect, as absurd as it sounds." Cole shook his head. "Currently in Kansas, there's an APB out for a septuagenarian WWII veteran who likes to steal 4-door rental cars."

Julia nearly choked on her sip of beer, laughing. "You never did answer my question this morning. How are the

Knox's?"

"Tim was being released today," Cole said. "His father will be in there for a few days yet, but it looks like he should make a full recovery."

"That's wonderful!" she said. "Did you speak to them about what happened?"

Cole nodded. "Same story as yours, basically. Kids with knives and black eyes came in, stabbed the father and knocked Tim unconscious."

Julia finished her beer, signaling to Pete that they were both empty. "And the second incident?"

"Not much to tell that you probably haven't already heard from Devin," he said.

Devin had given Julia a brief synopsis of the interactions with Jerry and Detective Cole earlier in the day while she'd waited for her film to process. "Devin said that Jerry saw one of them taken."

Cole nodded. "Yes, a group of kids pushed her into a car and drove off."

Pete appeared at the table with their drinks. "Food will be out shortly, guys," he said before disappearing back behind the bar.

Julia leaned forward. "What happened to them?"

Cole winced. "They bled to death. Slowly."

Julia felt a shiver run up her spine. "My God," she whispered.

Cole studied her. "I know I said this was completely on the record," he said, "but promise me you're not going to go out to the scene alone to get photos."

Julia nodded. "Of course."

Pete appeared next to the table and set a bubbling hot pizza on the table between them. "You guys need any parmesan?"

They shook their heads. Cole took the serving spatula and dug out a piece, dragging cheese across the table and to the plate in front of Julia. He repeated the action for himself before he spoke. "I looked into your brother's disappearance," he said.

Julia started, dropping the fork she was using to cut her pizza into bite-sized pieces. "Sorry, what?"

"Gene's disappearance," he said. "I told you I would look into it, and I have been."

Julia shook her head. "You mean in your spare time?"

"Well," he said, picking a pepper off his pizza and blowing on it to cool it. "I have a theory that it's connected to what's happening here. Black-eyed kids were at both scenes, so it has been worth it to me to go back in the records to see what I could find, both for his case and for this one."

Julia set her food aside, suddenly unable to eat. "And?"

"Well, there weren't a ton of witnesses. Evidently a couple truckers were still in the diner when it happened. They saw kids fighting in the parking lot and ran out to stop it."

Julia nodded, looking down at her untouched plate, stomach dropping slightly. "I've seen the news report. He was almost there to stop the fight when the other guy found my father and shouted. He looked away for a second, then looked back and the kids, and Gene, were gone."

Cole continued. "So, like I told you the other night, I went down the rabbit hole of black-eyed kid stories. As I'm sure you know, there are a lot of them." Julia nodded. "The ones that had places and dates, I cross-referenced in my super-secret detective database, and there's a common thread."

Julia leaned forward, eyes wide.

"More often than not, someone, usually under the age of 18, goes missing around the time and place of the black-eyed kid sighting."

Julia sat back, taking a deep breath. "So, some of these sightings where no one was hurt or taken, they were probably just botched attempts at kidnappings?"

Cole nodded. "Then they moved down the road or to the next township and *didn't* botch the attempt."

"So what do you think is happening?"

"I think it's a cult," Cole said.

Julia frowned and took a bite of her pizza.

"It's been around for decades, and strangely under the radar, but I think it's gaining traction because of the internet," he continued. "There haven't been any records of the sort of ritual sacrifices we're seeing here, but that doesn't necessarily mean it's not the same cult."

A tingling sensation had started in Julia's fingers and her face felt flushed. "So," she said carefully. "You think my brother was taken by this cult?"

"Yes," Cole smiled. "I think there's even a possibility he's still alive and traveling with them."

Julia pushed her food aside again. "You think he became a black-eyed kid."

Cole sobered. "Well, I don't mean…" he trailed off. "Look, I just think that it's the best, most logical, non-supernatural explanation."

Julia nodded, looking up to get Pete's attention. She gestured that she wanted the bill and the bartender saluted. "So what about the old guy?"

Excitement flared in Cole's eyes and he leaned forward. "Boyd Mingus. I went back into his records and he wasn't the most savory sort. His father was some sort of tent revival guy in the 20s and 30s, till he wound up dead near Chicago. That left Boyd an orphan who was in and out of the system, a runaway who got pinched a time or two pickpocketing and running low-level scams in his early teens. He dropped off the radar for a few years, either straightening up his act, or getting good at it. Then he joined the Army and supposedly died overseas. But the timeline almost matches up in terms of when the sightings began and when Mingus died, which we know he didn't, because we have his prints taken this week."

"Just so we're on the same page here," Julia said. She felt anger welling up and couldn't put her finger on why. "You think a guy faked his death in WWII and has since been Pied-Pipering kids into wearing black contacts and indiscriminately murdering and kidnapping."

Cole caught on to her frustration, setting his jaw. "How is that any less feasible than demon children?"

Julia felt like she'd been slapped. Was he right? She opened her mouth, then closed it, trying to squash the doubts that started pouring in.

"Julia, I'm sorry," Cole said. His face softened and he reached for her hand, stopping short by an inch. "I didn't mean to upset you."

"No, it's fine," Julia said. She stood, reaching into her bag and pulling out her wallet. She tossed a twenty onto the table. "I should go. I've got to write a story for my editor by tomorrow afternoon."

Cole stood with her, putting his hand on her arm to stop her leaving. "Julia, look, I know how you feel."

"Do you?" she snapped, shifting so he wasn't touching her any longer. "How exactly do you know how this feels? I lost my brother fifteen years ago, thinking he was taken from me by force. Now you tell me that he's lost of his own volition. How do you know how that feels?"

"My wife," he said, his voice had an odd quality, thick and rich.

She looked up, some of the indignant fire waning. "What?"

"She's been gone for five years." His eyes were cast

down, settling on the table. "One morning she was just gone. No signs of struggle, no note, nothing." He looked up at her and she was shocked to see anger in his eyes, and more stunned to realize it was directed at her. "She could be dead. She could be trapped in someone's basement. She could be on a beach somewhere with a fake name and new boyfriend. I have no way of knowing, and it's very likely that I will never know, what happened to her. So yes, Julia, I know how you feel."

Julia set her jaw, her own anger, spurred by her pride, rushed forward to meet his head on. Cruel words played around her tongue, threatening to spit forth into the tense air between them. She swallowed. "I have to go."

Cole closed his eyes, inhaling deeply, anger in his voice replaced with exhaustion. "Just promise me you won't go out to the scene of the murders alone."

She offered him a tight smile, saying, "I'll be fine," before turning and heading out the door.

Bash was having a late lunch at a cafe on the beach. His morning had been spent perusing the local shops on the main drag near the boardwalk. A used bookstore that hadn't been organized in at least a decade had been a pleasant diversion, and he'd purchased a couple books on recent US history before he left. The gift shop had a perplexing amount of t-shirts and mugs with the palm of a hand printed on them. He'd squinted at the little "you are here" star slightly below the pinky for a full thirty seconds before the bored teen behind the register had taken pity on him and held up his hand, palm out. "It's because the state is shaped like a hand. It's lame, but people seem to love it." He had left the gift shop without buying anything. There was a music store selling compact discs and a video rental shop that rented digital video discs for one, three, or five nights. He'd left those empty-handed as well, making a mental note to add "discs" to the list of things he had to make it a point to understand sooner than later.

He was engrossed in his book about the civil rights when the waitress slid his food across the counter. His burger was a few minutes past well done, and the lettuce seemed dubious, but the diner itself reminded him of his earlier days. The waitress was friendly, and she chatted animatedly with the customers. The cook peered through the service window, partaking in the conversation, which explained his overdone burger.

"Did you know about that?" asked the waitress.

Bash shook himself, drawing his attention to the conversation. "I'm sorry, I'm new to town, what are we talking about?"

The cook's head popped up above the wall. "That old marina, they're gonna tear it down."

"That marina is a hazard," gruffed an older man sitting at the other end of the counter. "It's been falling apart for years, collecting riff-raff and trouble-making kids, one of 'ems gonna get hurt. Plus, it's way too far north for where the tourists are coming in these days."

"Everyone likes the boardwalk," said the waitress.

"And who wouldn't with service like this," said the older man, giving the waitress a broad smile.

The bell above the door rang, ushering in a wave of people. "School's out," the waitress called back to the kitchen as the wave broke into smaller groups and found tables.

Bash turned back to his burger, finishing the last few bites. The hair on the back of his neck was standing on end, but he assumed it was just the sudden influx of people sitting behind him. He gathered his books and tossed a generous tip on the counter.

"Thank you, sweetie," called the waitress. "Make sure

you come back and see us again."

Bash gave her a smile, nodding as he left the cafe.

The man had taken a seat by himself in the corner, part of the throng of the after-school rush, and opened his laptop. The voices had started almost immediately, indistinct, talking over each other. Nervous, and angry. He put his head in his hands, trying to focus. They were talking about someone in the restaurant, but he couldn't catch why.

"What can I get for ya, darlin'?" the waitress appeared at his table, smiling down at him.

He stuttered, looking at the menu above the counter. A young man in his early to mid-twenties stood from the counter then, grabbing a cloth bag from the bookstore, and a leather jacket from the back of his chair. The waitress called a goodbye to him, then turned back to the man. "French dip is today's special, that sound good?"

The man nodded absently, turning back to his computer as it connected to the cafe's internet. The voices had temporarily quieted, and he was left with the stark white words on the computer screen. He read, allowing the words to fill his silent head.

The story was vague, somewhat hesitant. The writer had been followed home by black-eyed children, taken to a warehouse and nearly burned alive. It mentioned a young man who had helped to thwart the attempt, but left out the death of her roommate.

The man smiled softly and began to type.

# CHAPTER EIGHTEEN

Julia was not sober.

After leaving Cole at Charlie's, she had gone straight home and poured herself a tall glass of whiskey. She had glared at it for a few minutes before tossing a couple cubes of ice in the glass, as though "on the rocks" made day drinking hard alcohol acceptable. She had had another, not bothering with the ice, within an hour after that, stewing on Cole's brilliant deductions.

A cult. Like Gene would have allowed himself to be taken in by some creepy cult. Like he never would have tried, in fifteen years, to contact her. Gene would have fought his way out, even at twelve. Even as a depressed, angsty pre-teen who had lost his mother and his father...

She had her head in her hands when Bash walked through the door. She looked up, focusing on him before opening her mouth.

"You were in Kansas, weren't you?"

He shut the door behind him, then he set a bag down on the coffee table, before finally meeting her at the kitchen counter. He eyed the bottle of whiskey that sat on the counter next to her before speaking.

"I've been to Kansas many times," he said.

"A couple days ago." Julia narrowed her eyes. "You stole a car from the hotel and went to Kansas, then you left the car there and took the train back to town."

Bash cocked his head to the side. "Why would you assume that?"

Julia sighed heavily. "I saw your train ticket."

Bash frowned. "Still some pretty big leaps to-"

Julia held up a hand. "Don't fuck with me," she said. "I'm really done being fucked with. I want some straight answers."

Bash took a breath, pressing his palms against the cool granite of the counter. "Are you going to turn me in?"

Julia scoffed, an amused chuckle. "No, of course not."

He relaxed slightly, sitting back in his chair.

Julia continued. "I just want to know why your prints belong to an 80-year old World War II veteran."

Bash was very still for a moment before he answered. "Because I fought in World War II, in Germany in 1945."

Julia searched his face, looking for the lie and not finding it. She felt the effects of the alcohol scurrying away to saner pastures. "Can you explain to me how that's possible?"

Bash smiled, tilting his head, "To be honest, not really."

Julia stood, grabbing a glass from the cupboard, tossing some ice in it, and splashing a shot of whiskey into it before handing it to Bash. "Okay, we'll start smaller. What do you know about the black-eyed kids?"

Bash took a sip of his drink. "They're bastards."

"Do you think they're a cult?"

Bash laughed. "A cult? No, not as such."

Julia sighed, feeling her understanding of reality shift back into place. Gene had not spent the last fifteen years as a cult member. That was not a possibility, and maybe Bash could help her prove that.

"So you've dealt with them before," Julia stated.

Bash nodded, staring at his glass. "Where I'm from, they are…" he paused, frowning. "a problem. Definitely know how to crash a party."

"Where you're from?" Julia looked up, eyes narrowed. "Tennessee?"

A corner of his mouth turned up. "I am originally from Tennessee," he said. "But I mean more recently."

Julia watched him as he finished his drink, debating on pushing for more answers. He set the empty glass down and reached for the bottle, but she stopped him. "Nope, you're driving."

### \*\*\*
# From the Message Boards

## Topic: Grand River BEKs Part 2

**Forgotten1968** *4-11-2000 4:13pm*
Don't worry, Julia. You'll get another chance.
\*\*\*

The sun was low in the sky as they drove along the beach heading north. Sunset colors were already reaching up from the water, reflecting into the sky and turning the world a burnt orange. North of the boardwalk the town seemed to fade away quickly. They passed what Bash assumed was the old abandoned marina the folks at the cafe had been talking about, then the road turned inland.

Soon after, they were driving through wooded sand dunes. The light from the sun didn't reach over the dunes and through the tall beech and maple trees. Bash found the switch for the headlights and turned them on.

Julia didn't say much in the car, aside from giving Bash directions. It was a welcome reprieve. He'd been caught off guard by the accuracy of her accusations. He couldn't decide if he'd been out of the game too long, or if she was just that good. Given her apparent genetics, and his pride, he was more willing to believe the latter.

"There's a turn off to the left up ahead," Julia said.

Bash nodded, seeing the road that cut into the lakeside dune and taking the turn. It was a steep climb, but halfway up the dune, the road stopped at a small parking lot. Bash pulled into a spot covered in sand and turned off the car. "Now what?" he asked.

Julia grabbed her camera bag from the back seat. "Now we hike," she said and exited the car.

At the south end of the narrow parking lot, there was a rudimentary stairway made with rotting railroad ties sunk into the sand. The spacing was awkward, one step and a half to reach the next tie, but Bash found the rhythm before too long and was able to keep pace with Julia.

"This path isn't used much anymore," she said. "The boardwalk links to wooden stairs that climb the dunes closer to town. People seem to prefer that." The steps ended and Julia turned down an overgrown trail that went off to the right for a bit before she stopped abruptly and began climbing up the dune. "Almost there."

Bash followed, pulling himself through the shifting sands using tree trunks. It was only about ten feet up, but when they reached the top the light shifted dramatically. The sun was visible again and had just touched the water.

Sunset hues cast long shadows around them, lighting up the plateau they now stood upon. On the lake side of the dune, trees fell abruptly away to dune grasses and smaller bushes fighting against the wind and sand coming from the shore.

"It's going to rain soon," Julia said, looking out over the lake.

Bash turned his gaze, seeing heavy clouds to the north and west. "Well, then we'd best get done with whatever it is we are here for," he said.

Julia nodded and shifted her focus to the plateau. Bash saw it before she did. Deep red stains in the sand. "What is this?"

Julia saw it, and the color drained from her face. "The black-eyed kids took two more people," she said. "They're dead." She took her camera out of her bag and began shooting the scene. Wide shots of the whole thing, and then close-ups of the dark spots in the sand and the holes dug where the cleaning crew had tried and failed to rid the scene of the gruesome evidence of what had happened.

"Why are they doing this?" Julia asked, her gaze leveled on him. "What are they trying to accomplish?"

Bash shook his head. Something from far back in his long, long memory was sparked, but it wasn't matching up quite right, it didn't fit. "I don't know."

The clouds rumbled, moving south to obscure the remainder of sunset, and throwing the plateau into darkness. A shadow on the dune on the shore side below them caught Bash's eye. He squinted in the dim light, feeling his heart rate jump. Two shadows. A distant flash of lightning confirmed his suspicions.

Two pale faces, black eyes fixed on him and Julia. They stood still and silent for a brief moment, then leaned forward, grabbing onto shrubs with white fingers, and began to haul themselves up the dune.

# CHAPTER NINETEEN

"We have to go now," Bash said softly.

Julia was putting her camera in her bag and looked up at him, confused. "We've still got time before the storm," she said, looking out at the clouds.

Bash reached out, grabbing her hand and pulling her away from the edge of the plateau. "Listen to me, Winters," he said. "We have to go. Now."

His tone kicked her adrenaline into gear, and she nodded, letting him push her back down the dune. When they hit the path, they ran along the narrow trail to the steps. She paused to adjust her footing on the too-big stairs and glanced up to the plateau where they'd come from. She froze, and Bash followed her gaze.

"Shit," he hissed.

There were four of them, standing at the top of the dune and looking down at them. One by one they began to lower themselves down to the narrow trail.

Bash took her hand again. "Julia. Now."

Her petrification melted and she began to run, leaping down the steps with an agility that was born of self-preservation. When she hit the last step, her foot folded in under her ankle, preternatural agility dissolving into searing pain. She swore loudly.

Bash was there seconds later, pulling her arm around his shoulders and helping her to the car. It wasn't far, but they were severely hindered by Julia's ankle, and two of the four kids were nearly caught up to them by the time they made it to the car. Bash dropped Julia at the passenger side and turned toward the advancers. Julia saw him reach behind his back, as though expecting a weapon to be holstered there and coming up short.

"Get in the car," she shouted at him, opening the door and leaning in. She opened her glove compartment and pulled out a pistol, then leveled it at the closest would-be attacker. "Bash, get in the car, now."

Bash glanced back at her, then back to the kids who had halted their advance ten feet away from them. A beat later, Bash set his jaw and moved quickly to the driver's side of the car. Julia lowered herself into her seat, keeping the weapon trained on the hooded figures. When she heard Bash start the car, she drew herself in and shut the door just as he put the car in reverse and peeled out of the parking lot.

In the side mirror, she saw the kids melt back into the shadows before Bash turned onto the broken road down the dune.

Cole ducked, a futile attempt to avoid the pouring rain, as he ran from his car to Julia's apartment door. His knock prompted voices inside, muffled, but mostly distinguishable.

"Your cop friend?" said a male voice.

"Detective," said Julia. "Check the through the peephole, if they don't have black eyes, it's probably safe to open the door."

"It's me," Cole called.

The door opened a moment later, revealing a damp and slightly bedraggled young man that Cole had never seen before. "Detective," he said, and opened the door further to let him in. The man shut the door behind him, then found his way back to the counter with Julia. She was sitting on one of the stools, holding a cold beer to the foot that was resting on the stool next to her.

The stranger spoke again, gesturing with his own bottle to Julia. "Will you take a look at that foot and explain to her that it's broken and she needs to go to the hospital? Maybe she'll listen to you."

"She won't," said Cole, not smiling. "I sent two cruisers up to the old dune path. Hopefully they find the kids that chased you."

"They won't," Julia said. She winced as she moved her leg. Cole could see a dark bruise on the side of her foot which was well past swollen. "And no, I'm not going to the hospital. I'm fine."

"Suit yourself," the stranger said, shaking his head and taking a swig of his beer. He set the bottle down, empty, and stuck his hand out to Cole. "Sorry, pal. I'm Bash. Nice to meet you."

"Bash," he said, shaking the man's hand, but looking at Julia. "Bash the transient, Bash?"

Julia's face flushed, and Bash coughed a laugh into his fist. "Yeah, sorry. I meant to tell you. Bash is my new roommate."

Cole set his jaw, saving that conversation for another time, and looked down at her foot again. "Do you have a first aid kit?" he asked.

Julia nodded. "Bathroom closet."

"I got it." Bash got up and headed down the hall.

Cole took her foot, bending the ankle gently up and to the sides. Julia winced but didn't cry out. "I don't think your ankle is broken, but with this swelling, and that bruise, I wouldn't be surprised if there was a fracture somewhere here," he said touching the top of her foot.

"Yep." She sucked in air, biting her lip.

"That's what I told her," Bash said, pulling ace bandages out of the first aid kit.

Cole took it and began wrapping Julia's foot. "So who wants to tell me what happened?"

Bash opened another beer. "There were four of them, hanging out in the dunes near the crime scene. They saw us and gave creepy, methodical chase."

Julia nodded, winced, and then smacked her hand on the table. "Damnit, I had my camera *in my hands*! I can't believe I didn't think to get a photo of them."

"I think the gun was a more successful deterrent than the camera, Winters." Bash said.

Cole jerked his head up, staring at Julia. "You had a gun?"

She sighed. "It wasn't loaded," she said.

It was Bash's turn to look at Julia in shock. "It wasn't loaded?"

Julia shook her head. "My aunt gave it to me a few years ago, but I don't believe in guns, so I've never bought bullets."

"Are you kidding me?" Bash asked, anger suddenly apparent in his tone. "You pulled a gun on those bastards without bullets? You're insane!"

Julia grit her teeth, glaring at her roommate. "It was better than the *nothing* that you were going to defend us with."

Bash's eyes flashed, "You could have gotten us killed."

"It worked, didn't it?"

Bash sat back in his seat, head cocked to the side, silent for a long moment before he said, "Yeah, Winters.

Yeah, it did…"

His statement trailed off, and Cole wondered what thought the man was saving for later. He tightened the bandage, securing it. "How's that?"

Julia nodded. "Better, thank you."

"I would stay off of it if I were you," he said. "Not that I expect you to listen."

Julia smiled at him, sweet and innocent. "I've got my pictures and my story for the paper, no need for me to go anywhere for a bit."

Cole gave her a skeptical look, but let it alone. "I've got to go take care of a few things at the station," he said. "Are you going to be okay?"

She nodded, "We got away, I'm good."

"I'll call you if my officers find anything tonight."

"Thank you," Julia said. She set her empty bottle down and pulled a new one from the carton. "Tell Devin I'll call him as soon as I am drunk enough to put weight on my foot."

She met his glare with a wink, and he shook his head before nodding his goodbyes and leaving. He could hear Bash lock the deadbolt behind him.

Once in his car, he called the station. "Hey Biggs, can I get an emergency fingerprint check when I get back there?" Carefully, he pulled the empty bottle Bash had left on the counter out of his deep jacket pocket and deposited it into an evidence bag. "I've got a hunch I need verified."

"Winters." Bash was settling himself back down at the counter across from her. "I don't think these kids are the real thing."

She watched him for a second before he continued.

"Since when would a gun stop them?"

"I think a gun would slow anyone down," Julia said.

169

He shook his head. "Not black-eyed kids. Not even a little." He searched her face for a moment. "You've seen them before, haven't you? The real ones."

Julia's memories flitted back fifteen years without her permission, showing her images of a cracked skull and black blood. Gene's tire iron had done nothing to slow the advance of the monster that had killed their father.

Bash continued. "Nothing stops them, nothing slows them down. I've seen them keep coming after being nearly cut in half, still strong enough to kill." His face was stark, somewhat haunted.

"Where?" Julia asked. "When?"

"Far away," he said, "and relatively recently."

Julia took a breath. "How are you nearly 80 years old?"

"Because I was born in 1921."

"How is that possible?"

He gave her a rueful smile. "There are many theories as to how I came to be born," Bash said. She scowled at him and he laughed, finishing his third beer and went to the cupboard to pull down the whiskey. He raised his eyebrows at her, and she nodded, giving him leave to grab two glasses. He poured them both two fingers of whiskey, straight.

He sat back down and looked at her expectantly. "Where should I start?"

Julia listened to Bash tell his story. A story so fantastical, so far-fetched, that she wasn't sure she should believe it. A story about a young man who went to war, an attempt to do something right after a life of theft and scams. About bombs falling and facing certain death, but when he woke, he'd found himself in a new world. A town constrained by invisible borders. A forest where no one aged, but where they fought an almost daily struggle against the black-eyed kids. As he talked, he aged, not physically, but she could see the strain of decades pour over his face, memories painfully drawn out with the help of the whiskey.

After a long moment of silence, he looked up and smiled. "Oh, and I can hear dead people, too, but that's relatively unrelated to the rest of the story."

She studied him, watching him try to shake off the memories. "This is all true?" she asked.

He sobered, looking her in the eye. "It's all true," he nodded.

"How long were you in that world?" she asked. "Disonia?"

Bash's eyes went wide a moment, "To be honest, I have no idea." He took a drink. "I saw a couple kids leave the forest, go into town, grow up, grow old..." Another drink. "I was there for a while, I think."

"How did you get out?" She asked. "You said it was impossible."

"It was," he said. "There was a big dust-up, Carvy did a thing. An opportunity presented itself and I took it."

"Carvy?"

"Yeah, my war buddy, but he wasn't that guy, not anymore." Bash pushed aside the whiskey. "The deeper I go, the more I'll have to explain here, Winters. But basically, I think Carvy had a hand in making the world, and I think he had a hand in changing it at the end."

"How did he 'make' a world?" Julia asked.

Bash laughed. "We were holed up in this burnt out farmhouse, both of us too wounded to go much farther, and the bombs were dropping. He told me that he knew a girl who could help him create a new world, and he showed me this little figurine of a woman that he'd carved. I figured he had a few screws loose, but who was I to deny a dying man his delusions. I could hear the bombs coming closer, and it was nice to pretend there could be an escape, even if it was completely improbable." He shrugged. "It worked."

Julia's head buzzed with information, questions, and a little too much alcohol. She was having a hard time sorting out what to say next. The clock above the stove told her it was well past time for sleep, and she yawned thinking about her bed.

"I'm afraid to go to sleep," she told him, surprised at her own candidness. "I have all these questions, and I'm afraid you won't tell me any more when you sober up."

Bash grinned, "That's just a chance you'll have to take, Winters."

She rolled her eyes and hopped off her stool, shouting when her injured foot hit the ground. She staggered, but Bash was there to keep her from falling.

"Pretty good reflexes for a drunkard," she said in lieu of gratitude.

"Would you believe I used to be very much against alcohol?" he said, helping her limp to her room. "Dark, dark times, I tell you."

Julia laughed, opening the door to her room, leaning heavily on the door frame. "I got it from here, thank you."

Bash nodded, letting her go and touching the brim of an invisible hat. "Good night, Winters."

She grinned. "Goodnight, old man."

He gave her a look that, even in jest, made her realize that she never wanted to be on his bad side, then winked and disappeared through his bedroom door.

Devin couldn't sleep. He sat on his couch, watching late night television, trying to talk himself out of being terrified. Around sunset, he had taken Jerry to the police station and then stopped by Julia's, but no one was home. Dejected, he'd driven home.

The street had been quiet but for the pouring rain, but between the car and the front door of his apartment building, he had the awful feeling of being watched. Shadows loomed in the alleys on either side of the street, and he was almost afraid to peer too closely. Feeling like a child racing to hide under his blankets, he'd thrown open the entryway door, and fled up the stairs. He fumbled with his keys, glancing back down the empty stairwell. He couldn't see the door, but there was a square of light where the street lamp shown through the front window, and he saw two shadows flit by. He dropped his keys, then scooped them up, looking back down to see the two shadows back, human-shaped, standing stationary. Then he heard the handle on the entryway door rattle.

The key finally worked and he practically fell through the door to his apartment. He slammed it behind him and locked the doorknob, the deadbolt, and then the chain lock for good measure. His heart had just started to slow down when he heard footsteps coming up the stairwell.

"It's just the third-floor neighbors," he muttered to himself, but he could not tear his eyes away from the door, backing away from it and into the living room.

The footsteps stopped outside his apartment. Shadows falling in the slight gap between the floor and the bottom of his door. He squeezed his eyes shut, willing them to keep going.

The knock that came was slow and deliberate.

"We don't want any," he yelled.

"We just need to use the phone," came a girl's voice.

"Our car died, we need to call for help," a boy's voice this time.

"I don't have a phone, sorry," Devin called. "Check the party store a block down."

"Please help us," said the girl. "It's raining and we're cold."

*What the hell is wrong with you?* He thought to himself. *There are kids in peril outside and you're basically shitting yourself. Jerry has gotten into your head. They're just kids.*

Another voice in his head reminded him, It was "just kids" that kidnapped Julia and tried to burn her alive. He nodded to himself, agreeing that that was a fair point. A few moments later, he heard them move away, back down the steps.

He had picked up his phone, punching in Julia's number, but stopped short of the seventh number. He didn't want her worrying about him. He'd set the phone back on the receiver and went to the kitchen instead. His hands had shaken while he poured himself a drink.

Hours later he held the watered down remains of that drink in his hand, and stared blankly at the television, waiting for sunrise.

# CHAPTER TWENTY

The pain in Bash's head hit the second consciousness outweighed the middle sleep he'd been drifting in for the past hour. He groaned, unwilling to open his eyes to face the terrible sun that streamed through his window. His mouth tasted like gasoline soaked cotton balls, and a tiny monkey with cymbals began its routine in his skull. Despite the severity of the hangover, Bash didn't have any missing spots in his memory of the night before. He had told Julia about Disonia, some of it at least, and she seemed to believe him. There was still more to tell, however, and he was really not sure how she would take it.

Reluctantly, he opened his eyes. As expected, the light came through the window at an angle that told him it was mid-morning. He untangled himself from his blankets and stood, stretching. The apartment was quiet, so either Julia had left for the day, or she was still asleep and blissfully unaware of her own impending hangover. He got dressed and made his way to the kitchen. He started the coffee and scanned the sparse contents of the fridge for anything that looked like a hangover cure. He came up empty and was debating a little hair of the dog when he heard a shout from Julia's room.

A string of cursing floated down the hall as he hesitantly reached her door. "You okay in there, Winters?"

More cursing followed by, "Yeah, I'm just hungover and unable to walk."

Bash tried not to laugh. "Can I help?"

A moment of silence, then a reluctant, "Yes."

He opened the door to find her sitting on her bed. Sweat beaded on her forehead, and her foot looked like it had been slammed in a car door. He opened his mouth, but she cut him off.

"If you tell me to go to a doctor, I'm evicting you."

He shut his mouth, instead offering a hand for her to help herself up. "Can I talk you into some aspirin for the pain, at least?"

"Dear God, yes," she said, leaning into him as they walked toward the kitchen. "Lots and lots of aspirin." She disengaged and hopped to a stool at the counter, setting her leg up on the one next to her.

Bash went to the freezer, pulling ice cubes from the dispenser and wrapping them in a dish towel. He tossed it onto the counter and proceeded to pour each of them a cup of coffee. Julia got up again, using the counter to help keep her steady as she made her way around to the kitchen sink. She reached into the cupboard above, and pulled down a bottle of aspirin, popped open the cap and swallowed three of them dry. She gagged, turning on the sink and leaning over to sip some water from the running tap. Bash watched her, amused, and took the medicine bottle she wordlessly offered him after wiping droplets off her chin.

She then hop-limped back around to the dining room

side of the island counter and pulled her bag off the dining room chair. "I've got yesterday's paper if you're interested." She hopped back into her seat and reached into her bag, pulling out the paper and set it on the counter in front of Bash's cup of coffee.

He looked at the paper, bemused. "Thanks," he said. He set the aspirin back in the cupboard and took a seat, opening the paper and sipping his coffee. Julia took the camera from her bag and turned it on, pushing buttons on the back. Bash glanced over and saw that the pictures she had taken the night before were displayed on a screen on the back of her camera. He raised his eyebrows. "Things have changed," he said, shaking his head.

Julia laughed. "I imagine," she said. "Wait till you see the internet."

Bash was about to say something when Julia gasped, eyes wide. "I got a picture of one! The bastard was in the treeline behind the crime scene!" She turned the camera so Bash could see. It was hard to make out on the tiny screen, but there was definitely a figure in the woods in the background of her image.

"I'm still not sure they're the real thing," he said.

Julia frowned, looking at the picture. "That's something we didn't really talk about last night," she said. "What do you know about the black-eyed kids?"

He smirked. "I'm sober now," he said. "Feelin' less chatty."

She glared at him and he held his hands up in surrender.

"Okay," he said. "I know they could come and go from Disonia as they pleased."

"Really?"

"Yeah, they would walk to the barrier and just disappear. Usually in pairs." Bash took a breath. "And

when they came back, more often than not, they had
someone with them."

"What?" Julia asked. She felt her heart thump.

"They brought in kids usually," Bash said.
"Sometimes adults, but-"

"Jesus," Julia said, cutting him off. "That guy on my
website was actually on to something."

"On your what?" Bash asked.

Julia dismissed him, shaking her head. "This crazy
guy, he's always saying that the people who disappeared
with the black-eyed kids were 'taken to a better place.'"

"I wouldn't say a *better* place," Bash said. He opened
his mouth to tell her the biggest piece of information
when a knock at the door halted him.

Julia's brows drew together. "Who is it?" she called.

"It's Cole," the detective called back.

Bash stood and went to the door, unlocking it and
opening it wide.

The detective looked at him solemnly. He was flanked
on either side by a uniformed police officer. "Boyd
Mingus," he said.

Feeling a sharp stab of betrayal, Bash let out a breath
and looked back at Julia. But her expression was
confused, and she stood, limping toward him. "What's
going on?" she asked, seeing the officers.

"He stole a car, Julia," Cole said. He looked guilty for
a moment, but it was quickly masked by a stern
bureaucracy.

She frowned as the officers stepped in, putting cuffs
on Bash. "What do you mean? What evidence do you
have?"

"I ran his prints, they match the ones we found on
the car, the wallet, and the knife."

Bash saw a rage well up in Julia that he recognized
well. The last time he'd seen it, he'd found himself being

pinned and nearly choked to death by her big brother. He almost felt bad for Cole, but feeling the cuffs tighten around his wrists behind his back quickly quelled the sympathy.

"The 80-year-old man's prints?" she asked.

Bash raised an eyebrow, surprised to see her covering for him. "Yeah, Dick," he chimed in. "Do I look like an old guy?"

Cole set his jaw. "Take him to the station, I'll be there soon."

"You can't do that," Julia said. She put her hand on Bash's arm, holding him in place.

"Julia," Cole said, his voice plaintive.

"Detective," she said coldly.

"Hey," Bash said. "Don't worry, Winters. He'll take me down to the station, ask a second opinion about my age, and have to let me go when he realizes that eighty-year-olds don't look this good." He looked down at her, concern evident in her expression. He gave her a smile, then winked, "I'll see you soon."

She let him go and turned her gaze, furious again, back on the detective. Bash's smile shifted to a smirk as the cops led him away, leaving the detective with the full brunt of Julia's ire.

Cole stood on the other side of the threshold, but Julia wasn't letting him in.

"What the hell do you think you're doing?" she asked.

"Julia," he said, holding his hands out in front of him. "He showed up at the same time these kids did. For all we know he's one of them."

"He's not," she growled.

"You've got to see reason here. He could very well be the leader of this cult." His voice was pleading. "You've only known him for two days."

179

"Right, see reason and trust you, whom I've known for a whole week." Julia's anger hit a level that made her forget about the pain in her foot. She took a step back from the door, grabbed the knob and slammed it closed, for fear of what she might do to him if she let him say another word.

Fifteen minutes later she was pulling up to the Photo Shack. Devin met her at the door, having noticed her limping across the street.

"What happened, Jules," he asked, taking in her limp, as well as her general aura of anger and discontent.

"Did you bring pie?" Jerry asked from his position next to the counter.

"Does it look like she's got pie, Jerry?" Devin asked.

"Cole arrested Bash," she said, feeling her anger threaten to dissipate into helplessness.

"What?" Devin asked. "Why?"

"He thinks he's the leader of some giant, decades-old cult of black-eyed kids," Julia said, she looked up at her friend. "The real story is so much more complicated, but you have to believe me, Bash isn't the bad guy here."

Devin put his arms around her, hugging her and kissing the top of her head. "I trust you, Jules," he said. "We'll figure it out."

"Did you tell her about them kids trying to get into your house?" Jerry shouted at them.

Julia pulled back. "What?"

"I'm fine, nothing happened." Devin leaned casually against the counter.

"You told me you almost shit yourself," Jerry added helpfully.

Julia shook her head. "I don't have time or patience for any more bullshit, Devin," she said. "Just tell me what happened."

~ ~ ~

The front doorbell dinged, drawing Cole's attention away from the handcuffed man standing next to his desk. A girl, young, eleven or twelve, wearing a worn and well-loved backpack, walked purposefully to the front desk.

"I'm looking for Detective Cole," she said in a clear voice. Biggs glanced back at him and he nodded. The girl caught the exchange and met his gaze before striding across the room to his desk. "Hi," she said. "I'm Raccoon. I think I have some information about your case." She swung her pack around and began digging through it. She pulled out a laptop. "Do you guys have internet I can hook up to? If not, I've got a file folder," she pulled a thick folder full of loose papers from her bag, "but the laptop would be easier."

Cole noticed Bash turn to watch the girl with brows raised and shock written on his features. When the girl took notice of him she dropped the folder to the floor and froze still as a rabbit scenting a wolf. She stared up at him, eyes wide, face pale, for an almost uncomfortable amount of time before Bash finally spoke.

"Hey," he said. "How's your sis?"

Cole thought he saw tears spring to her eyes before she blinked them away and whispered, "Bash?"

"Yep."

"You were dead."

Bash shrugged. "You were shorter."

The girl's posture crumbled, her face flushing into a smile before she threw her arms around Bash's waist, squeezing tightly.

The girl pulled back. "It was you!"

Bash's brows drew together. "Not the best thing to shout in the cop shop, kiddo."

"No, I mean, you're the guy that saved the admin. Julia is her name, I think?"

Cole leaned forward, intent.

"She doesn't like it when I say I saved her, but yeah." Bash grinned.

"That explains a little, though I still don't know how you took down three of them."

"You and me both, squirt."

"Why are you handcuffed?"

"He stole a car, among other things," Cole said, drawing Raccoon's attention finally.

"Borrowed, if anything," Bash said.

"Illegally," Cole said. "Now I'm sorry to interrupt whatever is going on here, but you came here to speak to me about my case? Which case, young lady?"

She shook herself, gathering her papers from the floor. "Yeah, sorry. The case with the black-eyed kids."

Cole raised his eyebrows. "Is that right?"

"Yes," she said. "No internet, huh?"

Cole shook his head.

"Okay, well here's printouts of everything," she started leafing through them, handing select ones to the detective. "There's a website that's run by the woman that was kidnapped and escaped."

"Julia," Bash offered.

"Right," Raccoon said. "And there's a man that's super creepy, always commenting about how great these black-eyed kids are, and how they are actually taking people to some kind of heaven."

Bash chuckled. "She mentioned him this morning."

"Yeah, well," she pulled one more sheet of paper, handing it to Cole. "His messages have always been creepy and weird, but yesterday he posted *this* on the story about what happened to her." She pointed to the paper.

"Don't worry, Julia. You'll get another chance," Cole read aloud, frowning. "I'm not sure I understand."

"She never uses her real name on the website, she has a screen name." Raccoon drew out another piece of paper and handed it to Cole. "So I thought it was extra weird, and decided to dig deep and see who this guy was." Cole glanced at the sheet, it had a name and address on it. "And he lives here in town."

Cole frowned. "That's an odd coincidence, sure, but-"

"Julia is in danger," Raccoon said. "He's behind this, and he's coming for her again, I know it."

Cole looked from the girl to Bash, surprised to see that the color had drained from the man's face. "Are you sure?" he asked Raccoon.

She nodded. "Sure enough to hop a bus in the middle of the night to get here. My parents are going to be super pissed."

Bash looked at Cole, sober and serious. "Detective, let me go."

Cole shook his head. "This just seems a little too convenient," he said.

"Call her at least," Bash said. "Please."

Cole sighed, picking the phone off the receiver and punching in Julia's home phone. After six rings he hung up. "She's not home."

"Would she be with Devin?" Bash asked.

Cole picked up the phone again, dialing in the number for the Photo Shack. Devin picked up on the third ring.

"Photo Shack."

"Devin, hey, it's Cole," he said.

"Oh, Dishy," Devin said, gravely. "You are in trouble this morning."

"So I take it Julia is there?" he said.

"Oh yes, and she's hopping mad," Devin said. "Or just hopping, because of the foot thing." He yelped in pain. "I would not advise speaking to her unless you're giving her exactly what she wants."

"I don't think I can do that," Cole said.

"Well, that's unfort-"

Devin stopped talking, and Cole could hear the front doorbell ding on the other end of the line. A second later there was a loud thump as the phone hit the counter. He heard a scream, and then Devin yelled, "Oh my God, Jules!"

Cole's grip on the phone tightened as he heard sounds of struggling, shouting, and crashing. He stood, checking to make sure his gun was holstered.

Bash and Raccoon had been watching him closely.

"They're there, aren't they?" Bash asked. Cole nodded, reaching for his keys to unlock the cuffs, but Bash was already setting them, open, on his desk. "Let's go."

# INTERLUDE – FALL 1994

Elizabeth's knuckles were white on the steering wheel.

"Did we make it?" Rachel asked. Her eyes were wide and worried.

Elizabeth felt a lump in her throat looking at her little sister. She still looked so young, so innocent, but she'd seen so very much in the last... how long had it been? "I don't know yet," Elizabeth said. "If we did, I'm sure we will know soon."

The girl nodded. She looked down at the Donald Duck comics in her lap, flipping through them before turning her attention to the landscape outside the window of the old grey sedan. The land was flat, interspersed with overgrown corn and wheat. A sign for a truck stop came into view ahead, proclaiming that there were "Good Eats" five miles down the road.

Elizabeth smiled. "I could go for some good eats, how about you?"

Her sister nodded, "Definitely."

A few minutes later, the truck stop appeared on the horizon. There were cars in the parking lot. Elizabeth was afraid to hope as she pulled into a parking spot. She opened the glove box and grabbed a twenty from the stack of bills that were stashed within. She shut it and reached for her sister's hand.

The little girl looked up at her, "Where do you think we are?"

Elizabeth shrugged, not voicing the bigger concern of *when* they were.

They walked together across the dusty parking lot and were greeted with smoke and laughter when they opened the door to the restaurant. Two large men were sitting at a Formica counter, sipping coffees and smoking cigarettes. A group of black-haired teens were holed up in a corner, huddled over their own cigarettes as though worried a parent may come in and see them smoking.

Elizabeth found them a booth near the door and sat, then hopped up again when she noticed a newspaper lying on the counter next to the men. "Can I borrow this?" she asked.

"Sure can, sweetheart," said one of them, giving her a genuine smile before turning back to his companion.

She took it back to their table hurriedly, flipping to the front page. "We're in Oklahoma," she told her sister. She scanned to the top of the page, seeing the date and feeling tears well up in her eyes. "And it's only been six months."

"Good afternoon, ladies," said the waitress as she appeared at their table. "My name's Pam, what's yours?"

Elizabeth was almost overcome with emotion, but she swallowed it down, smiling at the woman. "I'm Elizabeth," she said. "This is my little sister, Rachel."

Rachel frowned at her, shaking her head before she looked up at the waitress. "My name is Raccoon," she said. "And I would like some French fries."

# PART THREE
## INTERLUDE - 1968

"Oh my God, Patty, did you see that?" Christopher danced from streetlight to streetlight, filled with the thrill of having seen the best movie ever. "They're coming to get you, Barbara," he said, "then bam! Dead people walking around and eating people! That was amazing!"

Christopher paused in his glee, looking back to see his little brother meekly following along behind him. He backtracked and slung an arm around the nine-year-old. "Patty, you can't tell Mom that I took you to see that, okay? She'd tan my hide." He turned the boy to face him. "See, she doesn't know how grown up you are, she thinks you're still just a baby, but we know better, right?"

The boy's angelic young face looked up at his big brother. "I'm not a baby," he mumbled and began walking alongside his brother. "But Chris," he said, stopping again to look up at the teen. "It *was* scary, a little bit."

"Yeah, Patty," his brother smiled down at him. "It was definitely scary, a little bit."

A fog began to gather as they walked out of downtown and into a low-lying residential area. Houses were dark at this time of night, and street lamps were spaced far apart. Away from the brightness of the marquee, the movie didn't seem so entertaining. Even Christopher was starting to let his imagination get the best of him after ten minutes of walking, seeing flesh-eating ghouls hiding in the mists and shadows.

"Hey Patty, you wanna race home? It's only a couple more blocks."

The younger boy shook his head, "No, you'll leave me behind!"

"I won't, I promise," Christopher said. "Ready, set, go!"

The older boy sprang into action, running a full house length before the younger of the two was able to coordinate enough to start. "Chris!" he yelled after his brother, seeing him disappear into the fog. "Chris, wait up."

"Keep running, Patty," came his voice from up ahead.

"I am!" he yelled, pumping his little legs as fast as they would go.

He heard his brother shout right before he came into view again, only this time he was not alone. His brother had fallen onto the pavement and was crab crawling backward, away from two figures that were advancing on him. It was difficult to make out features. They wore hoods, and the boy thought he saw a flash of silver in one of their hands.

"Chris!" he yelled, freezing in place. He saw one of the figures reach his brother, bending down to pick him up. When it threw Chris over its shoulder, the younger boy charged forward, yelling. He ran headlong into the creature that was carrying his big brother.

It was like hitting a brick wall, and he found himself

landing hard on the ground. The second attacker was on him a second later, no emotion in his jet black eyes as he started slashing at the boy with a long silver knife. He put his arms up to protect his face and felt the blade sear his skin from elbow to wrist. He screamed, flailing. The second creature stood, joining the first. They both turned their backs and began walking into the fog.

"Chris!" the boy yelled, he staggered to his feet. "Chris, you said you wouldn't leave me behind!"

The shadows disappeared into the darkness, and the boy fell to his knees, sobbing and holding onto his injured arm. He felt a twinge in his arm and in his head and he heard an alien voice speak to him inside his mind.

*"He's going to a better place."*

# CHAPTER TWENTY-ONE

The Photo Shack door was open when they got there, a rack of specialty photo paper had fallen and wedged itself between the door and the frame. Bash was out of the car and pushing the door open before Cole could put the car in park. There was blood on the floor. A lot of blood.

Raccoon came in right after him, followed immediately by Cole.

"Miss, you might want to wait in the car," Cole said, drawing his weapon.

Bash looked back, seeing Raccoon roll her eyes. "She's seen worse, detective."

A second later, a blinding headache tore through his skull, followed by a voice.

*"Them kids,"* it said. *"Took them both. I tried to stop 'em..."*

Wincing, Bash started scanning the store, trying to find the source. He followed a trail of blood back behind the counter and found an old man, dressed in rags, crumpled on the floor. A wheelchair rested on its side a few feet away.

He leaned down, closing the man's eyes. "Do you know where they went?" he asked softly.

*"I tried. Didn't want them to get took. They were nice to me."*

Bash felt Cole round the counter behind him, "Shit, Jerry." The detective pulled his phone from his pocket, dialing.

"You did good," Bash said, realizing the man probably had no idea where they were taken. "It's not your fault."

"Yeah, I've got a stabbing victim at the Photo Shack on Main, I need an ambulance,"

*"Them kids,"* Jerry's voice was fading in Bash's mind. *"Riff-raff and troublemakers. I just wanted pie…"*

Bash put his hand on the dead man's face. "He doesn't need an ambulance, detective."

*"Riff-raff and troublemakers…"*

He stood, and Cole bent down, checking the old man for a pulse. The voice was gone, but the words started banging around in Bash's consciousness, connecting dots.

"I think I know where they might be," he said.

"Were you talking to him?" Cole asked. "I think he's been dead since before we came in…"

Bash's temper flared. "I said, I think I know where they are. Do you want to interrogate me on my methods? Because they don't have time for that shit. I will take your car, leave you here, and go rescue them myself, do *not* test me."

"I've got his keys," Raccoon chirped, pulling Cole's keys from the pocket of her oversized, well-worn hoodie.

"Jesus Christ," Cole said, snatching the keys from Raccoon and moving toward the door. "Who the hell are you people?"

Julia thought she might be drowning. That was the most

feasible explanation. She could hear water, great wooshing waves, and she couldn't open her eyes. She was afraid to draw in a breath, for fear the waves would fill her lungs.

"Julia wake up, please."

Devin sounded very far away. She opened her eyes and saw him peering at her from the end of a deep tunnel. Maybe she was in a well, fallen down a well, call the papers.

"Julia?" his voice was pained and desperate. "Jules, please."

Julia fought against the water and the fog, chancing a deep breath, relieved to find air filling her lungs. She gasped again, feeling her head clear. She looked at Devin and saw him rushing toward her until reality snapped back into place and she was able to assess the situation.

The sound of waves had not been in her head, the smell of the lake hung heavy in the air along with rot and mildew. Her arms ached, and she realized they were tied above her head, her feet, bound together and suspended in the air at least five feet above a rotten dock that moved with the water. Devin was next to her, hanging from the same fallen crossbeam that had wedged halfway between the ceiling and a series of crumbling docks against a support beam and the wall. She started kicking her legs, ignoring the pain in her shoulders and broken foot, but Devin halted her.

"Jules, we knock that loose, we fall into the water and probably die, or even better we might bring this whole building down on top of us."

To illustrate the point, the support beam shifted slightly, causing debris from the ceiling to rain down on them. Once the onslaught dissipated, she gently turned herself to face him. "Good point," she said, then looked him up and down. He had a split lip, blood still trickled onto his chin. "Are you okay?"

He blinked at her. "Relatively? I mean, apart from everything happening currently, I'm good."

"Sorry," she said, trying to unscramble her thoughts. "I can't... wait." She started looking around their surroundings, frantic, but careful not to shake their crossbeam.

They were there. Of course they were. A row of them standing on the shore side of the docks. Behind them was a wall of cracked and dirty glass, letters emblazoned backward toward the top confirmed that she was in the abandoned Grand River Marina, far from anyone who would hear their shouts above the noise of the wind and the waves.

She searched their blank faces, looking for signs of humanity, but unable to see clearly in the dim light coming through the dirty windows. She craned her neck to see the opposite end of the marina. Huge doors that spanned from the top of the building, stopping ten feet above the water were rusted closed by the looks of it. Under them, the water swirled and spun, hinting at the deadly currents that raged underneath. If they dropped into the water, they would get sucked under the docks and into huge rocks that she knew lurked below the surface.

"Still with me, Jules?" Devin asked. His face was so pale.

"I'm here," she said softly. "Just trying to plan our grand escape."

"Right," he said. "Water is death, creepy kids blocking the door have knives and already killed Jerry, and that's conveniently ignoring the aforementioned issues with even getting off this beam."

Julia's heart ached. "They killed Jerry?" She felt tears sting her eyes, and saw that Devin was trying valiantly to hold his own back.

He nodded. "He got in their way, trying to save us, I think."

Julia took a breath. "Okay, well, let's not die then. For Jerry."

Devin choked on a cross between a sob and a laugh. "For Jerry."

"Who is this guy?" Cole asked Raccoon as they sped down the shoreline out of town. "I didn't get a good look at you print-outs."

"His address is listed as being owned by P. Hudson, a 40-something male," she said. "I couldn't get a first name. After that last post on the message boards, I didn't want to waste too much time. I stopped digging and got a bus ticket."

"Good girl," Bash said, throwing a half grin to the back seat.

She smiled back at him, feeling a strange nostalgia wash through her, tempering the adrenaline that had been building since they got to the Photo Shack. "How much longer?" she asked Cole.

"Five minutes," he said, putting his foot down on the gas as they hit a straight stretch of road. "Maybe less."

"Bash," Raccoon asked, feeling her voice shrink like it used to when she was small. "Is it them? Are they here, too?"

Bash thought for a minute and then shook his head. "Not these guys. They're not strong like the ones in Disonia." He reached back, patting her knee in a comforting gesture. "We can take 'em."

Raccoon cleared her throat and gave him her best "no shit" expression. "Well, yeah, I know that. I just wanted to know how long it was going to take. I gotta call my parents when it's all over."

~ ~ ~

*"Hurry, hurry, hurry,"* said one voice.

*"Get us home. We have to go home,"* said the other voice.

The man peered through a clean spot in the window and saw that the photographer and her best friend were where he'd ordered the kids to put them. He felt the voices mumbling to each other, just out of his reach.

He opened the door, nodding to the kids as they turned to look at him. He glanced down the dock, seeing that the lines that held their victims were tied off on a support beam right off shore near a slightly more stable dock.

He followed the line back out above the water, gaze landing on the pair. The girl stared at him, incredulous and angry.

He nodded at her, face grim. She'd been nice enough, but once they had gotten a taste of her, the voices wouldn't have had anyone else.

"Well," he said aloud. "Let's create a new world."


"Do you know him?" Devin asked, seeing the look on Julia's face when she caught sight of the apparent ringleader.

"No," she said. "Yes. I mean…" The man nodded to her, and turned to the kids, saying something she couldn't hear above the waves. "He's the counselor at the high school," she said. She squinted, trying to focus on the faces of the teens around him, horrified to recognize the four kids she'd photographed the day before. "Bash was right," she said. "They're not real."

"They're real enough," Devin said. "And I think they're going to cut our ropes."

The man, Patrick Hudson, was gesturing to the ends of the ropes that held them above the water. "Okay, so the plan is to survive being dropped in the water with bound hands and feet," she said. "It's dug out to ten feet or more here in the marina. There are rows of giant rocks underneath each dock, and the eddies are going to push us down and into them."

Devin nodded. "And it's going to be cold, it's all ice melt this time of year."

A tall boy with a machete started down the next dock toward their ropes. She turned, meeting her best friend's eyes. "We can survive this, Devin. Deep breaths. Prepare for the cold shock."

"Curl up in a ball, hands over head and pray for a good, non-bone shattering angle into the rocks." Devin started taking his deep breaths, seeing the boy closing in on the ropes, drawing the weapon back to strike.

"Hold your breath, hope for buoyancy," Julia said. They locked eyes again. "I love you. I will see you soon."

Devin gave her his best attempt at a smile. "For Jerry."

And then they were falling.

# CHAPTER TWENTY-TWO

Bash crept into the marina through a broken window, Cole and Raccoon close behind. The adult, P. Hudson, held court in front of eight fake black-eyed kids. Julia and Devin were hung suspended above a half-rotten dock, hands and feet bound. To his right, Raccoon followed shadows down to the edge of the water, pulling on a rope that was attached to a flat-bottom boat being tossed around in the waves. To his left, a couple easy-target stragglers were standing apart from the group, watching the older man make his speech. He was sliding toward the first straggler when the man's voice reached his ears.

"...make a new world?"

All those nagging almost-theories clicked into place. They were trying to recreate what Carvy and his unseen girl had done. *Would it work? Am I about to get sucked into another Goddamned Disonia?*

He got to the first straggler, reaching out to tap his shoulder once he was close enough. The kid turned, mouth opening to shout before the right hook struck his temple, silencing the warning. Bash caught him as he crumpled, lying him gently to the ground before he moved on to his next target.

He was nearly close enough to take her out as well, when the gunshot rang through the air, immediately followed by the sound of splintering wood and a splash that to him sounded even louder. The girl he was closing in on turned, but he raced past her, heading to the crumbling, splintered dock. His sole focus, the bubbles breaching the surface of the water where Julia and Devin had just been dropped.

As expected, the dock had shattered under them as they fell. Julia swore she heard a loud bang, and then she was under the water. The cold was like thousands of needles stabbing into her, and she had to fight hard not to open her mouth and gasp. She saw Devin for a flash, then he was pulled away through the murky water and away from her.

She quickly lost track of which direction was up, and she felt the slack of the excess rope floating around her. She hadn't thought of that and hoped that Devin realized what was happening before it got tangled.

She saw a wall of rocks and felt herself being hurtled toward them. She followed Devin's advice and curled up into a ball, praying for the best.

Devin was at the rocks a few seconds before Julia, swept ten feet farther from shore. The wall came up fast, and he wasn't able to curl up as he had planned, instead his bound hands came up instinctively to protect his head. Jagged rock tore into his palms, peppering the water around him with blood. He made a fist, clutching at the slick rocks, finally getting tentative purchase on a particularly jagged outcropping. He wrapped the excess rope around the base of the rock twice to keep him from slipping further away from shore, then planted himself as best as possible. Shoving down the growing panic in his lungs, he set about working the ropes that bound his hands across the sharpened edges of the rock. It was a thick rope, and he was running out of time, but passively drowning was not the way he wanted to leave this world. This desperate attempt was currently his best option.

All eyes turned on Cole after he fired the shot, too late, at the kid with the machete. He was on the ground, yelling about his wounded arm, but he had gotten his swing in first and now Julia and Devin were on borrowed time. The kids were all frozen, eyes wide with terror at the complication of a gun into the situation. Out of the corner of his eye, he saw Bash bolting toward the dock, but he was caught up short by the school counselor who grabbed him by the arm, spinning him around. Bash used the momentum to throw a punch to the man's solar plexus, but the counselor acted as though he didn't feel it. Bash looked at his face, shocked, and swung another punch, but the older man used it to swing Bash around, pinning his arm behind him. Quicker than was logical, the man had a knife to Bash's throat, holding the transient hero in front of him as a shield. Bash struggled but wasn't able to get leverage or purchase, and soon a rivulet of blood was staining the front of his shirt.

"They need me," the man, Hudson, shouted at Cole. "They're stuck here and can't get home. I promised I would help them create a better world." Bash struggled, wincing as the knife dug deeper. Cole caught Bash's eye, then glanced down at their legs as the man continued. "You have to let them die, they're the spark that will-,"

Bash nodded, then made his move.

Raccoon had already been paddling toward where Julia

and her friend went under before they had fallen. The boat was floating a few feet away from the trailing bubbles now. She found a life jacket and tied the longest of the straps to her belt, then tossed it over the side, diving in after. She wasn't prepared for the cold, but she fought past it, opening her eyes to search the murky waters. She caught a glimpse of something white and started toward it, but she didn't have much clearance before the life jacket started pulling her back up and she started running out of air. She breached the surface, refilling her lungs, then dove back down, kicking as hard as she could to reach the object she'd seen. Just as the life jacket began to win the war again, she saw it bobbing near her again, a coil of a rope that disappeared after about three feet in the dark water. She reached out, grabbing it and wrapping it around her wrist before she headed back toward the surface.

Using his left leg, Bash kicked back hard, half convinced it wouldn't work. The man was an adult, and he didn't have black eyes, but Bash could swear he had the strength of one of the bastards, and the close vicinity made Bash's skin crawl. The kick made contact with a satisfying crack on the man's shin. Bash twisted, moving to the side just enough for Cole to get a shot off, hitting the man square in the knee. He buckled, letting loose of Bash and falling to the ground, screaming.

Bash leapt away, letting Cole handle the rest and ran down as far as he could on the dock before it broke away to churning waters. Raccoon was a couple yards away, holding onto the edge of her little boat with one arm, and pulling on a thick white rope with the other, hiking it up a few feet at a time until Bash saw Julia's blonde head just below the surface. He dove in, crossing the distance quickly, and helped Raccoon get Julia's head above water.

She gasped as soon as she hit the air, and relief washed through Bash. He pulled himself into the boat, then grabbed Julia's bound hands, lifting her in as well. He turned to help Raccoon up, but she tossed him a pocket knife and shouted, "There's still someone down there!" before diving beneath the waves again. Bash took the knife, cutting Julia's hands and feet free. She stood immediately, bending to send herself back over the side of the boat, but he stopped her.

"We just pulled you out of there," he shouted at her.

"I can swim now, I'll be fine," she said. "Devin is still down there."

Before she was finished talking, Bash had looped the rope around her waist, tying a knot. He tied the other end to a handle on the side of the boat, making sure both were secure. "I'm right behind you," he said. She nodded and dove in. He waited for two breaths and dove in after.

Devin's vision was starting to darken, shadows creeping in around the edges as he slid the rock through the last fibers of rope. Free, the thought occurred to his quickly shutting down brain that he had no idea which way was up. Continuing with the string of desperate attempts, he let most of the air out of his lungs watching the bubbles as they scurried toward the surface. Once oriented, he stretched his long arms and started pulling himself in the same direction. He silently thanked Julia for forcing him to join the swim team in high school, even though he hated it at the time. The bound legs would have been a death sentence without that training.

His hands broke through to air, fumbling to get him above the surface before his lungs gave out. The air, warmer than the water, finally filled his lungs and his vision sparkled, then returned to normal. He treaded water, allowing himself some deep, measured breaths as he spun around, looking for any sign of Julia. A boat floated about twenty feet away, closer to shore, empty. The end of the dock, decimated from their fall, floated in pieces around him, traveling with the current out to deep water.

He saw Detective Dishy on shore, handcuffing the ringleader, but that celebration would have to wait until he found Julia. He had been swept so far from shore, he had to assume she may be nearby as well. He took a breath, stole himself and dove back under.

Julia pushed aside the pain in her arms and her lungs and followed the white strap to where the little girl who had saved her was struggling against the current and the pull of the life jacket. She saw Julia and shook her head with an exaggerated shrug, pointing toward the rock wall. Julia nodded and worked with the current, hoping it would take her to her friend. The rocks appeared fast out of the gloom, and she had to adjust her speed to make sure she didn't slam headfirst into one of them. Turning, she saw Bash coming up behind her, slowing when he got to the wall with her. The current was taking them further out, and the rope around Julia's waist pulled taut.

In the dim she saw a length of rope a few feet down the rock wall, floating ghostlike and glowing against the dark. She reached down, pulling at the rope around holding her to the boat, but Bash caught her arm and shook his head. She batted his hand away with a glare, untying the knot and pointing at the other rope further down the wall. As soon as she was free, she swam to it, relieved to see that Devin was no longer attached. Bash pointed to the frayed ends, then pointed up toward the surface.

The current was taking Raccoon further from shore than

she liked, she was floating parallel with the dock now, past the point where it had shattered, and into the debris. She was about to dive again when a man broke the surface five feet in front of her, panting and moving awkwardly to stay above water. A few moments later, ten or so feet to her right, Bash and Julia broke free of the lake. Julia cried out when she saw Devin, grabbing a large piece of floating wood, and swimming it over to her friend. The two of them started toward the dock, where Cole was waiting to pull them out.

Bash turned around in the water, spotting her and cocking his head to the side. "You need a hand, squirt?"

She was starting to move faster in the current, away from shore. "Bash, if you need to use my life jacket, don't be ashamed, just ask."

He laughed, closing the distance between them quickly, and putting his hand on her life jacket, pulled her in toward the dock.

Cole's hands were impossibly warm against Julia's frozen skin as he hoisted her onto the remaining sections of dock. She turned, helping Cole pull Devin out onto the dock so Cole could cut through the ropes wound around his ankles. Once free, her friend stood, wobbly, and cupped her face in his hands, kissing her before he wrapped his arms around her, squeezing tight.

Police began to enter the building, subduing the few kids that were left. Julia heard splashing behind and turned to see Bash hefting the little girl who had pulled her to the surface up into Cole's hands. She landed lightly on the dock and untied the life jacket from her belt. Bash lifted himself onto the dock with no help, shaking water from his hair in a spray that doused the front of Cole's coat. He grinned at the little girl, punching her shoulder lightly. "Nice job, kiddo."

Ambulance sirens joined the wail of the police sirens. "We should get out there and get checked out," Devin said. Julia nodded, and started walking, but buckled as she put weight on her foot. "Oh yeah, you've got a broken foot," Devin said. He crouched, putting his shoulder under her arm for support as they started down the dock and toward shore. "It's just not your week, is it?"

As they got closer to the handcuffed man, his whimpers turned into words. "No, please no. I didn't fail," he said. A choking sob and then, "Please don't, please. Give me another chance. I won't fail again."

Devin looked back at Cole. "Would you mind steadying Jules for a second, Dishy?"

Cole obliged, taking his place. Julia looked up at him, squeezing the shoulder where her hand had landed. "Thanks for coming, Cole," she said.

"Any time, Julia," he said, giving her a tired smile.

Neither of them saw what caused the handcuffed man to scream, but Bash let out a bark of laughter, and when they turned Devin was walking back up the dock with a pleased smile. The handcuffed man behind him doubled over and shaking, momentarily silent.

Devin nodded to Cole, who stepped back and allowed him to retain his position next to Julia. Once they were moving again, passing Hudson, he leaned down and whispered in her ear.

"For Jerry."

# CHAPTER TWENTY-THREE

Julia leaned on her crutches, avoiding the glare of the nurse who had given her a stern talking-to after seeing that she'd ignored her broken foot for over a day. The woman had wrapped her foot with a compression bandage, tsking the entire time. The horse pill the nurse had given her for the pain did little to dull the throbbing ache in her foot, but it helped with the soreness in her muscles and the sting where the ropes had cut into her wrists.

She saw Bash and Raccoon through the glass walls of the waiting room. Raccoon, who had introduced herself as "That girl who's always arguing on your message boards" before the ambulance had taken her, was sitting on a bench, animatedly chatting with Bash. Tiny, with her legs folded under her, swimming in an oversized hoodie, an ignored comic book open on her lap, a worn backpack tucked in next to her like a teddy bear. Bash looked tired but amused as he listened to her. He stood, patting her on the head as he walked by to get to the water cooler. She stuck her tongue out at him.

They stopped talking and looked up at her when she clumsily made her way into the room. Bash cocked his head to the side. "Foot broke?"

She scowled at him and found a chair to settle in.

"They've got Devin in for stitches," Bash told her. "Shouldn't be long."

Julia nodded, looking between the two of them for a moment.

"How old are you, Raccoon?" she asked the girl.

Raccoon blinked wide eyes at her. "Twelve...ish."

Bash returned to his seat, handing Raccoon a cup of water.

"How is it that a 12-year old and an 80-year-old war vet know each other?"

Bash closed his eyes, chuckling. "Well…"

"He used to uh…," Raccoon wrinkled her nose, "boink my sister."

Julia choked on a laugh, wincing as the muscles around her rib cage contracted.

Raccoon looked between her and Bash, eyebrows raised. "Are you guys…"

"No," Bash said quickly. "No we are not, and you are too young to…" he trailed off, noting the skeptical expression on the young girl's face. "Fair enough."

Julia shook her head. "But I thought you had just gotten… here," she said, unsure of the words. "I mean, out of-"

"How do I look?" Devin interrupted, sweeping into the room. He had a bandage over his bottom lip and chin, and his hands were covered in tiny cuts with bandages on them. He had gauze bracelets that matched Julia's. "I'm hoping for a sexy Harrison Ford-esque scar." He looked at Julia. "Oh! Crutches!"

"Hey guys," Cole looked up from his desk as Julia and

the others walked into the police station. "Thank you for coming. I just needed to ask a few questions and make sure I have as many details as possible."

"What," Devin said, pulling up a chair for Julia near Cole's desk. "You don't think you can convict him?"

"You just never know, honestly," he sighed. "One of the problems is that Hudson didn't actually lift a finger in any of the crimes. He ordered these kids to do it. We have eight of the kids in custody, and I hope that's all of them."

"So it was a cult," Julia said softly. She looked so tired. "Like you said."

Bash frowned, watching Julia pick at the gauze around her wrists.

Cole nodded, "That's what it looks like. I don't know how far-reaching, but hopefully I'll be able to get some answers once they release Hudson from the hospital."

"He's not here yet?" Devin asked.

"He needed some pretty extensive medical treatment," Cole said. "What with the gunshot in the leg, and then it seems that someone kicked him really hard in the gut and may have caused a little internal damage."

Devin nodded solemnly. "Shame."

Cole hid his smile and turned to Raccoon to begin the questions at the beginning.

"I mean, it's not hard to find someone on the internet," Raccoon was saying as they walked into Julia's darkened apartment.

"Would you believe she almost never talked when I knew her?" Bash asked Julia, flipping on the kitchen light.

Raccoon threw a small fist into his arm and he laughed. "That was a long time ago," she said.

"Not for me, kiddo" Bash replied.

207

Raccoon tilted her head to the side, her eyebrows drawing together. "When did you leave Disonia?"

Bash looked up at Julia, seeing realization dawn behind the exhaustion in her eyes.

"Oh," she said. "I get it…" She went to the fridge and pulled out jelly, took bread and peanut butter from the pantry, and a couple butter knives from the drawer, tossing them all onto the counter, mumbling to herself, "I think I get it. I mean, who can be expected to *get* any of this really, but yeah. You two were in Disonia together. Got it."

Bash turned back to Raccoon. "I left right after everything went down," he said. "But my route brought me here just a few days ago."

"Wow," Raccoon said. "We left right after as well, but we got here six years ago." She sat at the counter and began making herself a peanut butter and jelly sandwich.

"How long had you been gone?" Julia asked. She took a butter knife and began slathering peanut butter on her own piece of bread.

"Six months." She grinned. "I spent my summer vacation before first grade spending ten or so years in a different dimension. 'Lizbeth and I agreed not to tell anyone that part." She took a huge bite of her sandwich but didn't stop talking. "Our parents assumed we'd been kidnapped or something. Dad's a bigwig in tech, so he assumed it was all about him and his money, but it's not like anyone ever asked for ransom." She shrugged. "It was just easier to let them tell their own story. Neither of us wanted to end up in the looney bin." She took another bite, chewing it thoughtfully, turning her attention to Bash. "How long were you gone?"

Bash ran a hand back through his hair. "Well, I left in 1944, I think. Came back last week - so that was a while."

Raccoon shook her head. "No, I mean how long were

you in Disonia?"

He sighed, shaking his head. "Longer than that. Kinda lost track."

Raccoon nodded, finishing her sandwich, then yawned. "Sis won't get here till morning," she said. "Is it okay if I stay here tonight?"

Julia laughed. "Of course you can."

"I'll sleep on the couch tonight," Bash said. "You can have my room, squirt."

Julia set her sandwich down and grabbed her crutches, motioning for Raccoon to follow her down the hall to Bash's room. After a few moments, Bash crept down the hall and lingered in the doorway, watching Julia tuck the young girl in.

"I've got some old comic books if you want anything to read," she was saying.

Raccoon hugged her backpack close to her. "I've got that covered."

"Need anything else?"

The girl shook her head. "No, I'm good." Julia nodded and turned to leave. "Thank you, Julia."

Julia turned back, eyes wide. "You saved my life," Julia said. "Seems the least I can do is put you up for the night."

Bash left the doorway and headed back to the kitchen. By the time Julia joined him, he had two tumblers full of ice and whiskey ready for them. She settled into a chair at the counter and slumped over her glass, head in her hands.

"How's it going, Winters?"

She sighed, shaking her head. "Been a long day, old man."

He laughed. "Cheers to that."

They clinked glasses and were silent for a few long

moments. Bash, enjoying the peace, and Julia lost in thought. When she finally looked up to speak, her eyes were red. "It was a cult," she said. "My brother was taken by a cult." Tears started to well, but she blinked them away. "He's been here all along, and he never tried to find me."

"Okay, two things," Bash said. "One, this wasn't just some cult. That guy, Hudson, he was dabbling in something far beyond himself. I don't know how or why, but he had their strength. Fighting him today felt just like fighting those things back in Disonia. And he had this crazy idea that you could create a world by killing two people, which sounds to me like a bastardized version of how Disonia was created, right? He had some sort of skewed knowledge and power from somewhere."

Julia was watching him, tears gone and curiosity piqued. "Okay," she said. "What's the second thing?"

He set down his glass and leaned forward. "Julia, Gene is in Disonia."

The color drained from her face, "What?"

"Your brother," Bash said. "He's in Disonia. And he's been there a long time."

# CHAPTER TWENTY-FOUR

Julia woke the next morning feeling somewhat like she was living in a different world. The smell of bacon traveled down the hall, infiltrating her room, and giving her more motivation to rise and get her crutches. Her dreams had been vivid, and all of Gene.

Bash had told her Gene had spent some time with him in the woods, fighting the black-eyed kids, but chose to leave and grow up in town. He found a wife and got married. Lived in the fancy district, and opened a business in downtown Disonia, Gene's Arcade & Spirits. He had a daughter Julia's age that he'd named after her, Julie. "He was, is, a good man," Bash had told her.

Tears stung Julia's eyes again as she got out of bed. Her brother was alive, and well… and old… and stuck in a different dimension. The emotions were complicated at best, but the most powerful one was hope. She now knew, without a doubt, that she would and could find a way to see her brother again.

Raccoon was sitting at the counter with a plate of bacon in front of her, munching happily. She spun around when she heard Julia come down the hall. "You're Gene's sister?" she asked, grinning. "No wonder you're so nice!"

"You knew him too?" she asked, pulling up a chair and stealing a piece of bacon.

"Yeah! He gave us his car to leave Disonia," she nodded. "And a load of cash, and all my comics." She patted her backpack. "He was the nicest person I met in Disonia."

Bash gave a wounded scoff, tossing another batch of bacon onto the plate.

Raccoon looked at him. "Gene was, without a doubt, the nicest person in Disonia. You, Bash, were an ass."

Julia laughed, and there was a knock at the door. She stood, working the crutches around the legs of the stool to answer.

"Did you tell your sister I was here?" Bash asked in a hushed tone.

"Nope," Raccoon said, grinning.

Julia opened the door to see a tall, attractive young woman on the other side. Her eyes had dark circles and her brows were drawn together with worry. "Hi, I'm Elizabeth."

Julia nodded. "She's here, come on in."

The woman stepped inside, seeing her sister first and rushing over to give the girl a hug. "Why do you do things like this?" she asked. "If you would just tell me, then I can make up a better story for our parents and I can help-" she broke off abruptly when she looked up, seeing Bash behind the counter. "What...?"

She stood, walking slowly around to the other side, eyes fixed on him. He flashed a cocky grin at her. "Hey there, turtle dove."

She frowned, cocked her head to the side, and punched him square in the jaw.

# EPILOGUE

The darkness oozed through the hospital ward, announcing their entrance a full minute before their physical presence. The night nurse trembled, turning her chair instinctively away from the hall as they walked past. An orderly slipped into a patient's room, closing and locking the door before he cowered in the farthest corner. A guard, sitting half-asleep in a chair outside Hudson's door, found himself willfully immobile. He curled himself in a ball as they came down the hall, trying to be invisible.

When they were two doors away, Patrick Hudson began to wail. "No, please," he was moaning. "I can do better, I swear." A long wave of sobbing as the darkness thickened in his room. "I tried, I did. Please take me to my brother. To the better place, please…"

In Hudson's hospital room, two teenagers, a girl and a boy now stood silent, staring at him with dead, pitch black eyes.

"Please…" he trailed off. "I tried, I really did."

Knives appeared in the children's hands.

The nurse, the orderly, and the guard all covered their ears when he started to scream.

# ABOUT THE AUTHOR

Jen lives in rural Michigan with her daughter, husband, cats, dogs, and a small dragon named Milton.

# ABOUT DISONIA

If you want to know more about Bash, Raccoon, and the world of Disonia, visit www.disonia.com.